CW01657531

June '26

The Story of the Deer Woman

Dear Tracey,
Enjoy the Madness
+ the Magic,
♡ Heidi Handa
xx

First published February 2026

Published by
Lemon Jelly Press
Isle of Wight, United Kingdom
ISBN: 978-1-9191893-5-2

A catalogue record for this book is available from the British Library.

To my beloved Beki. Sweet sister of magic,
joy and beauty. I love you.

1.

The day she pricks her finger.

Once upon a time, we were all animals. And all animals lived on the land. Rolling about in the grasses and the muddy waters. Eating the leaves and fruits and roots and each other. Playing and loving and fornicating and birthing, in the ways that all creatures are wont to do. And then one day we became human. And we complicated it all. And we got too far away from listening, ear pressed gently down to the soil. We lost the art of wonder and enchantment and curiosity, sealing them in books to be read at night to soothe the soul of a child. Or we got lost in those strange landscapes both eerie and exotic as a balm for the sharp edges and misunderstandings of the world we inhabit. That is, until the world pivots once more and all is well again. Well. Maybe not well per se. But different. Yes. Everything is different again. And that is all you can ask for. And this is that story.

It was a moody, late autumn day, a Wednesday, when a sharp whip of the wind, which had propelled her without choice down the blustery wind tunnel that is Oxford Road, abruptly changed its mind, and direction, as if it had another plan for her all along.

It certainly seemed that way. These were unprecedented times. Apparently. Highly unusual. Unsettling and worrying. These times were discussed a tremendous amount of daily time by all members of society. From the save our earth activists, to the bespectacled science boffins. From the 'quick hide the money in our secret underground bunker palaces' politicians, to the conspiracy theorists all over social media. And from those visionary thinkers that spout big words with their awfully luscious red, strangely erotic looking, at least in her opinion, lips.

Closer to home you had the Jesus and apocalyptic believers, touting for God and salvation and attention with their large placards proclaiming the end of the world being nigh, pacing up and down Market Street, seemingly oblivious to the fact that the world seemed to have ended there quite some time ago.

Nevertheless, it was indeed ridiculously windy.

Reports of these strange winds had been flashing across weather maps for weeks now, blowing old ladies, small dogs, and unaccompanied children up into the sky like balloons floating away with the clouds. Reports of their whereabouts from Monaco to Seville to the Aegean coast flooded across the news channels. Everyone knew someone, or rather, everyone knew someone who knew someone, whose member of their family had been blown all the way from the rain-trodden and sodden streets of Manchester, across to the plazas and palazzos of Europe.

The wind was doing odd things to people's minds too. They would walk out of their house and immediately not remember why, or where they were going. They would stop halfway across the road wondering in which direction they were crossing, without even a chicken to ask them why; and they would stand clueless in the fluorescent lit, giant Tesco's on Market Street, wondering what on earth they liked to eat. Even those placard holding 'the-end-is-nigh' salvation groupies forgot their mission and put said boards down, their eyes turning to the pub across the street and the thought of a nice cold pint of beer bringing a thirst for living that the upcoming apocalypse had negated a long time ago.

For her, it was a restlessness. A longing. For something she couldn't quite reach out to touch, or lick, or smell, or taste, or hear. She felt a scratching in her soul, an itch she couldn't reach, not even with her beloved wooden back scratcher that she'd had since the age of eleven. A curious gift to give to a child but it was her favourite thing over that time. She loved the feel of the little wooden hand scratching against her skin. It tickled her and gave her a thrill that she secretly knew was not something to be spoken about, especially when she discovered places on her body that felt nice. Made her feel warm. It was hers. Her own private Idaho.

When nothing appeared to appease this restlessness, she'd taken up walking. All day on her days off. Through the city streets. Along the canals. Repeated loops of footsteps pounding the sodden Manchester pavements. Hell, she knew this city like the back of her hand. She'd lived there for over a decade. It was her backyard. Her playground. As she walked, she was lulled. Her feet kept time. But still. She was on the hunt.

Seeking something. But not knowing exactly what. For her, taking to the streets was instantly and immeasurably preferable to falling into and down an Instagram coma hole and the horror of only stopping when the feed ran out.

And so, this is how she found herself that day, walking down Oxford Road for the millionth time, past the grand-fronted University buildings. Though she couldn't say that she had chosen this route with purpose that day. Indeed, it did appear that it was the wind itself that was guiding her feet.

And so she walked.

Past the little park where the students hung out whenever the clouds had parted like some kind of summer miracle, eating falafel and ice cream, looking like the art students that they inevitably were; and past the Royal Northern College of Music, where slithers of glass panes revealed the serious matter of practising one's instrument of choice - the violin, the drums, the vocal cords and the soft sounding keys of the piano.

As it was, another change of the wind's mind whisked her through, and spun her around, the mahogany revolving doors, straight into the grand atrium of the Manchester Museum. It was quiet inside, the doors closing behind her the world of the busy city. Here, all was silent, dark, yet vibrant in anticipation of who knows what.

The air was morbidly still, which, whilst seemingly discombobulating at first after being outside, served to calm and hush her windswept mind and hair. Gliding past the huge, flying dinosaur skeleton, cases of the relics of fossil menageries, encrusted crustaceans, and multi-legged creepy crawlies, she found herself standing in the room that glorified the mammals and other creatures that had once roamed majestically and freely across the earth. Yet now, beheaded, and stuffed, their breath and hearts beat their pulse no more. Time stood still, as did she.

She was transfixed. And sad. A strange sepulchral melancholy hung in the air, causing her to hang her breath so that it draped in sighs every now and then as she peered at the animals closeted behind glass-fronted coffins, forever on display and frozen in time. The stuffed animals' eyes troubled her and appeared to follow her every move as she walked slowly around the room. She couldn't read their glazed expressions, and she felt a hunger arising from the pit of her belly, and a desire to converse with them and stroke their fur-pelted skins. But she couldn't, of course, and instead simply pressed her fingers, palms and upon occasion, nose, against the cold glass. She stayed here, her breath fogging the glass, misting her vision, adding to a sudden sense of dizziness; her fingers anxious to leave, a bone-deep aching in their joints which felt old, ancient; whilst her revulsion and compulsion kept her pushed up as close as it was possible to get the most from her front row viewing. She wanted to leave, yet something kept her body pinned in a stillness not unlike that being mirrored back to her - coated in frozen fur - from inside every glass case.

It was 3:47pm, just over an hour before the establishment was due to close for the night that the incident occurred. Running her index finger along the silver-embossed plaque in front of one of the exhibits, so faint and old in its wordings that she was unable to read it, a sharp, rusted nail scraped said digit causing her to flinch and pull back her finger. A single, fat drop of blood glistened in a round shiny ball and instinctively she placed it in her mouth to suck. At the same time, coincidence or not, she could have sworn that the deer head, so royal in its mount, winked at her.

The shock of pricking her finger combined with the animated eye of the deer without a body, caused her to make haste. So, she ran, like the proverbial wind, back down the corridor, back through the revolving mahogany doors, and back out into the street. Strangely, though she didn't notice such things as she made her way home rather hurriedly, the wind had disappeared, and all was calm.

Some might say, eerily calm.

And as all things are governed by natural laws, the eerie calm would, in time, whether one liked it or not, foretell the coming, and the becoming of, the storm. For her, this storm, in a teacup, would never ring so resonant.

2.

The introduction of the Immortal Woman.

The Immortal Woman saw it all. Or rather, she felt it all.

The moisture of the woman's breath against the glass. The sharp, pained *'ouch'* of her finger pricking upon the nail, and the vision of her own wide eye being reflected back in the globule of blood that appeared on her finger in response. And then the frisson of something undeniable, and familiar, that shivered, like an invisible electrifying eel, through the air between them, tapping into the space the Immortal Woman inhabited between life and death.

This was a space that changed and morphed, and where the laws of time defy themselves until they no longer make any sense. Well, apart from her. They make perfect sense to her.

And so, she watched with a mix of unsettling intrigue and narrow-eyed curiosity as the Deer Woman, as that is what she would be known as from now onwards, rushed from the atrium and towards the exit.

Then the Immortal Woman felt it. Every single part of her rising up as if to take the Deer Woman into her arms. She shuddered. This was a sensation that she hadn't been used to for a long time. For a very long time.

The Holy Grail whereby time stands still. An immortality that defies all logic, all reason, rhyme and cause. If we could be given the secret of eternal life, perchance in a gilded glass bottle with a stopper all pearl-dropped crystal, would we uncork it swiftly without mind and down its elixir with reckless and relief fuelled abandon?

She did. But not out of a bottle. For it was not a liquid that gave her the answer to man's unobtainable last mystery, but it was youth. The youth of others. The ones with their impossibly smooth and clear polished skin with its rosy fresh tint. The ones with hope and years in their eyes, of unfathomable endless life and possibilities. It was the ones who walked with a gait only the angels and gods could grant, careless and carefree and as light as the breath of the newly born.

And all it took, which had taken her by surprise the first time it had happened many, many years ago, was one touch. One touch. An accidental brush up against someone's warmth and neck, a graze of fingers upon another's slightly clammy fingers clumslly gripping door handles and bannisters. The slightest curl of an unfurling hair gone awry and astray so that it teased against her skin.

What she derived the most pleasure out of though, was the feel of their body, warm and strong, when pushed up and pressed against without apology, on those busy trains at rush hour. Now, a word here about said trains. You see, most likely a remnant echo of her aristocratic tendencies and fondness for a certain parlance of snobbery, she would only ride certain trains in certain cities. If she was essentially stealing the life force of others, then she damn well desired the best. The pedigree of life forces. The 4* Michelin dining carriage service, so to speak, par excellence. This could mean she'd happily spend a weekend becoming deliriously drunk on leather briefcases, tailored suits, expensive perfumes, and Italian brogues, riding the London Underground District and Circle line over and over again. By the end of those days, she looked sharp. Suited and booted with a slash of red lips, an eye for the filthy rich and the most luxurious of hotel rooms.

She'd tried the metro tram in Manchester. Twice to be clear. And each time, she felt a repulsion arise from her gut. The life force on offer there was not to her taste. Why eat at Subway if you're used to the best restaurants in the world.

Those Northern trains were not for her, and though she had no desire to live in London - it was too busy for her neurotic temperament - she did frequent the city for weekends of debauchery and delicious Tube revelry.

She would ride those trains back and forth for hours, like an addict, her hunger becoming more ravenous with each journey. The carriage would bounce, and sway, and she would go with it, and in the way that people are in such situations, paying no mind to this invasion of physical space, they would acquiesce to the inconvenience. The inconvenience, which these people believed to be of no consequence. And yet there were consequences. Every single time.

She could feel her life force returning as it was happening. She would feel a rush of what felt like liquid iron forcing its way through her veins, pulsing and pushing itself with vehement certainty, and with a confidence that upon occasion threatened to overwhelm her. It was as if she had been injected, brusquely and crudely, with God. With the spirit of the sun. With life itself. And she would gaze at her hand, the one that was held aloft gripping the loose hanging noose that apparently was all that one needed to survive a dignity whilst hurtling through underground tunnels at such abandoned pace. The lines on her skin would fade, ironed out, made smooth again, her flesh pumped up from the inside, from others' life.

She would feel her tits lift into a buoyancy fondly remembered, and sometimes fondly fondled, from her own, once lived in, youth. She could sense the tautness to the skin on her brow, her belly, her ass. And she could feel underneath the flesh of her newly revitalised form, a vigour and sweetness returning to her heart.

As for those she stole from. They wouldn't necessarily say that anything untoward had occurred upon their voyage. Their minds filled most often with thoughts from their busy days and busy lives; they were blind to this mockery and kidnapping of their own life. And yet they would find themselves more tired than usual upon return to their homes, their feet aching, their bones too, a dryness to their lips and eyes that for a moment might startle them before shaking it off as the effects of all that commuting. But their life had been stolen. There had been a theft, albeit unreported or even undetected. And minutes and moments had been taken off their lives. Who can say what that extra hour or day or minute would have meant to them or their loved ones.

Because of the gift of their life, though given unknowingly, the Immortal Woman never aged. By feeding upon these strangers, she remained youthful, bright, with a strength of mind and a virile vitality that kept her primed in a prime that had long since sailed away. And yet, this feeding upon others had become untethered. Now it was more akin to an obsession. An unreasonable compulsion. One course of enchanted action, that had begun so long ago that its beginning story had long since faded from the page. In many ways she no longer knew why she fed from people, but what she did know, without a shadow of a doubt, was that she never grew old.

Yet her mind aged. Curiously over time, and she had lost count over the years of exactly how much time, bored by her marking of days, and wondering what the point of all of this time meant anyways, she had felt her memories slipping away. Or they would become confused. Perhaps she wasn't only stealing these people's lives but their memories too. And she could feel these images that showed themselves to her. Feel the lover's hands and mouth on her body; feel the heartache of a father's death repeatedly shattering her own heart into glass shards; and feel the exhilaration of breath and the fire in her leg muscles of climbing to the peak of a mountain in Asia. She could also see and feel their shame, their guilt, their fears and jealousies, their hopes, and disappointments.

The last of these was the worst. Disappointment tasted like metal and overpowered her on a number of occasions. Bitter metal. It was the taste lingering far longer than any memory attached to it. She had to keep a box of cherry-flavoured Tic -Tacs in her purse to try to hide the taste when it rose up like bile in her throat.

She hated them then. She hated herself even more at those times and would curl up in a ball as waves of disappointment washed over her, taunting her and pulling at her hair and poking its fingers sharply and painfully at the spaces between her ribs.

Disgust was the one she feared the most though. But how could she tell? How could she know what the people carried as a secret, rotting their arteries. My God, they were all so young. How could disgust have tarnished their souls so soon? It made her tremendously sad, but not enough to stop. But disgust did make her more cautious over time. For you see it stayed, it lingered, like cigarette smoke, never quite leaving once it had nested and nestled itself between threads, hiding behind wool and stitch. Sometimes she would feel disgust curl its way into her ears and nostrils, even her mouth and disturbingly, not that all of this was not already disturbing enough, it would attempt to force itself between her legs, to push itself into her sex, into her womb, where it would curl up wrapped around itself, perversely feeling safe in the deepest darkest part of her.

She knew she was fucked, so to speak. It was only a matter of time, which in itself made no sense and made her laugh with disappointment's bitterness on her tongue. They would get her. It wasn't the falling failing of ageing's decrepit flesh. Nor was it the faulty faculties no longer functioning. But those memories and emotions that had taken hold of her for themselves after she breathed too long the flavour of a person's short life.

What could she do? Should she do?

She didn't know of any way out. Well, any way that seemed possible that is.

She held the secret to immortality, to endless life. Only her. She ached and yearned to feel the sweet treasures of youth as they poured into and through her. How her own blood felt like sugared syrup as it eased through her veins, hydrating her skin, her flesh, her bones, swelling her with innocence. She felt quenched, enlivened, renewed, and oh my, how she enjoyed the swift cleverness of her mind after she had fed. The wit of one who was not yet soured by the years falling away. She felt as if she was being given another chance at her life, over and over again. Yet sadly, she no longer recalled what to do with it.

They gave her life. And slowly they were taking it away from her too. A devil's bargain she supposed, and one that she had signed the paperwork for, the small print long ago disappearing into dust, along with the key to her freedom. Or so she remembered. Wrongly, as it turns out.

Yet, it had become as clear as a fresh new day, that another peculiarity of her gift was in the certain shifts in her physical appearance which caused her to be changed over time. Her waist narrowing. Her nose elongating. Her hair acquiring the colour of the darkest wood or the palest moonlight. These visible changes were often rather sudden and had caused a fright each and every time she had noticed such a thing. She still found herself spooked now and then, even after all these years. But a steady diet of, one might say, a healthy selection of different types of people, kept these changes to something that occurred more or less every seven years or so. When a change was rather radical, she would simply remain in the city she was living in, but either change her occupation, or as was the case in her current line of work - with the physical transformation being so alarming and dramatic - that she had immediately quit as the person that her fellow staff were acquainted with, citing an illness in her immediate family, causing an immediate booking of a one-way ticket home. Home to where she never did clarify. And then, as if by some strange fated act, a casual mention upon pretending to visit the museum for the 'first' time as this new woman - that she had just moved here recently to live with her sister and could she pass her CV on to someone in charge. Of course, her CV held the skills that were an exact match for the last person to hold such a position who had suddenly quit only a day prior to this one. Wouldn't you know it?! With an incredulous look that mirrored that of the person standing in front of her, she said that she could begin straight away and that she was already in love with the space. From what she'd only just seen of course.

And that's how she ended up working at the museum for thirty-seven years now. In one form or another that is.

She might be immortal but even the ones who meddled in such underhand matters needed to pay their rent, and one mustn't forget that she was rather partial to the finest things in life, so that was a need that required funding. And working in a place where her main role was to handle creatures that no longer had any life force left in them, was the most perfect place for her to be.

And the safest.

Or so she had thought.

For on this autumn afternoon, during the most unusual weather Manchester had seen in a while, she felt a stirring of hope, a sniff of the air, and a sensing of the scent of the Deer Woman's blood. And it was this latter that felt strangely elating; awakening something remembered in her own heart.

That was a feeling that she hadn't felt in many a year.

3.

An accidental meeting at the bookstore.

It wasn't difficult to track The Deer Woman down. As luck, or good fortune, would have it, at a charity event a few weeks later, an archivist who worked at John Rylands library, mentioned to the Immortal Woman, that the Deer Woman worked at John Rylands too, as a librarian. She was meant to have attended this event with the archivist but had mysteriously come down with the flu that very morning. So, the archivist was there on her own. That was until she got chatting to a middle-aged man who happened to be an actuary, and they spent the rest of that evening drinking wine, chatting, and then finishing the night off, disrobed and debauched, at her place.

With a little detective work - read stalking - the Immortal Woman soon discovered the Deer Woman's schedule. She had worked full-time at the library, until very recently that is, when she had begun to show signs of some sort of possible chemical or hormonal or mental or emotional imbalance that might be to do with the strange weather that had been toying with people's minds in all manner of confusing ways. *Poor thing*, agreed her colleagues, as they kept their distance just in case. Her manager agreed to her part-time hours without refute.

Discovering that the Deer Woman had an occupation similar in tone to hers pleased the Immortal Woman greatly. It seemed like both women had a taste for the textural quality of silence and that sacred hush of such public spaces that demand we pay attention to the curious and curiouser. It also alluded to the possible fact that both women were far more comfortable in the company and intimacy of the inanimate objects that they both looked after, preferring these to the company of other human beings, complicated irrational creatures that they were.

The first few times she took to frequenting John Rylands Library, the Immortal Woman didn't go near the Deer Woman. She knew that there was something dangerous about her, though not in an obviously threatening way of course. No. She was dangerous to her controlled - if you could really, truthfully, honestly, deem to call it that - existence, which, as illogical as that seemed, both scared and excited her; such an irresistible and fateful combination, and one that she rarely felt towards another.

So, she kept her distance.

Partly because she didn't yet quite know what she wanted from her or what to say to introduce herself. But mainly, she was quite aghast at the strength of the force that was coming off from the Deer Woman - a force which seemed to be growing more powerful each day. She didn't understand it, beyond the irrefutable compelling nature of it, and not willing to find out if her will was strong, or sane enough to take the risk of restraining the temptation to drain the life force out of her - she suspected not - she remained an anonymous customer. Feigning absorption in the artefacts and maps of the library's shop, or a particular book on an eighteenth century typeface, she could keep the Deer Woman in her vision whilst pretending to browse.

This was a hunger so immense that she could have sworn she could feel the chasmic void in her belly which the Deer Woman, unbeknownst to her, well, unbeknownst to both women as a matter of fact, had opened, all abracadabra-like, swirling with aliveness for another's life.

This too did very little for her, already unstable, mental balance. If she needed to be pushed off the edge, then this was the mere whimpering whisperings of a feather's touch, just enough to send her into an infatuation, that ultimately would be both the death of her and the freedom of her too. Of course, she didn't know that. And perhaps, maybe, you don't need to know that just yet either.

Yet it is worth noting that it hadn't escaped the Immortal Woman's attention that there was something odd happening in the museum recently. Specimens appeared to have changed their position, even their room, during the night. These frozen in shape and place creatures, poised as they were, always reminded her of life-modelling that she used to do a long time ago.

This was a profession that she had returned to over the years, the decades, the cities and the times that she'd lived through with a flaunt of a thigh, and an ability to keep the shape of a pose for longer than three minutes. She adored being a life model, and not just simply for the fact that her dress code, no matter the era, was always that of her own soft flesh. She got a strange thrill out of feeling her limbs going all pins and needles numb, shaking uncontrollably at times when a pose was held for longer than a certain number of minutes, even if that tremble was almost imperceptible to her acutely observing audience. It made her, albeit fleetingly, feel like a normal, vulnerable, flawed human being.

It was assuredly the most perfect job for her, especially whilst in certain of her nubile incarnations, as she could be around people, yet circumstances required of her not to be in too much physical closeness. And oh how she felt the shimmering seduction of this sensually inviting tease. She would while away the minutes posing like a living and quivering statue, listening to the silence of a room tempered only by the various sounds of gentle music and the scratching made from pencil upon paper, whilst feeling the tenuously taut pull towards the younger attendees who, so focused on their own masterpieces and that wondrous meditation that drawing gave, were oblivious of her hunger for them.

Of course, she would give in to such sweet, juiced temptations from time to time. A hand on an arm or shoulder whilst pretending to be interested in their drawing of her, as she breathed in the scent of their flesh, and felt the electric current of their life force smoothing out a wrinkle on her thigh. Though certainly a delight to dalliance in, she had hung up her career in such a field upon the realisation that maybe, just maybe, she had an unhealthy fixation for the whole damn scenario.

Now unexplainable occurrences were commonplace in such an establishment like the Manchester Museum, that deals with mummies, sacred vessels, thousands of years old fossils, skeletons of creatures now extinct, masks, and cabinets and cases containing amulets and tools for divination and other objects of wonder and rarity. Yet the feeling that she had, upon inspecting the glass-encased cabinet that housed the deer head that the Deer Woman had experienced so much time with before fleeing in such dramatic fashion for a midweek afternoon, left her feeling puzzled and uneasy both. The animal had felt alive to the Immortal Woman. She could feel a pulse of life current. Faint, for sure, but it was there. Of course, no one else would even suspect or notice, never mind pick up on such a thing, as other humans' sensibilities were not as sensitively developed as hers were, but there was no doubt that this deer head, as ludicrous as it sounds, was alive. Did she cause this to happen? Was it possible that whereas the Immortal Woman took life, the Deer Woman could give it? She had to find out.

She had to make their meeting a chance. One of those serendipitous points of time where two people are fated to meet because the gods ordained it so. Yet, she wasn't a God, far from it, and so she had to be clever. Perhaps, instead of a God, she was a trickster, a fool, someone who played with one's sense of what was right or wrong. Certainly, her morals were beyond questionable at this point in her life. So, she would need to be artfully cunning, to make their meeting simply a synchronicity.

She'd noticed over the last few weeks that the Deer Woman had a particular routine, a pattern that created loops of time that were familiar. Habits. She'd leave her work on the two days that she frequented the library at 5:10pm on the dot and head down Deansgate towards the canal. Sure, it was winter now, a fact that Manchester seemed to embrace with glee each and every year. It was dark. And yet the Deer Woman would disappear down the steps to the canal religiously and walk the narrow path alongside the canal boats with their steamed windows and smoke from their wood-burning fires rising up to the sky, and the smell of burning wood and coal filling her nostrils as she passed by.

The Deer Woman walked hurriedly, as if attempting to escape from something, or someone, chasing her. The Immortal Woman always kept enough distance for her presence to seem normal, even though other anonymous shadowy figures were few and far between at that time of the year, bar the joggers, and the youth who were heading to one of the bars down at Castlefield. As these young people passed her by, for she walked amongst the shadows herself, the Immortal Woman would catch her breath, stirred by their scent, and more than once she had to restrain herself from reaching out to touch one of them. She ached to stroke a cheek unburdened by the lines and frowns of the complications of living. She was even startled to feel a rising urge to lick the ear of a particular youth who, busy chatting with friends, was oblivious to this strange behaviour and want.

No. This canal business was not going to lend itself to a fruitful encounter, she realised. Even more so, she could sense that a life lived in the shadows of the canal at night, was both reminiscent of the lure that she felt fondly from her days in Victorian London, and a one-way ticket to her tenuous mind tipping over into dizzying dissolution. And so, she stopped following the Deer Woman in the evenings as she took her canal sojourns.

And yet, maybe fate was curious too. Or perhaps it was bored with the usual goings on and so it decided to choose the following Sunday to play with a fire that destiny could smell, like the scent of sulphur from a blown-out match.

The Immortal Woman was wandering around a bookstore. One of her often-visited places, she sought refuge in the stories and worlds of others. Just like the museum, here was a place for tales to live for all time.

Or at least until someone picks that particular book up and chooses to take it home with them.

She felt safe here. It was peaceful in Waterstones on a Sunday afternoon. She could manage to keep away from others, or, very rarely, she would deign to pass her hand over another's, reaching for the same book from the same shelf, laugh it off with some great British fumbling embarrassment, which made her cringe, whilst feeling that ripple of electric run through her veins as her cheeks flushed and the skin on the back of her hands ironed itself out.

She always felt this abhorrence afterwards. As if the idea of her stooping so low to find life, was revolting to her very aristocratic marrow.

On that day though, her fortune changed as she was perusing the latest offerings in the Japanese author section. Narrow-mindedly and shockingly so for someone seemingly well-versed in culture - not simply through life's experiences, but also literally through feeling what it was to be that person - she was partial to what she perceived to be these authors' 'simple' observations and 'odd perspectives' on life. It was whilst browsing the manga section of the store, which always drew in the ones with the porcelain skin, huge wide eyes and Influencer Tik-Tok personalities, that she started to feel that familiar feeling. The one she'd had that day when she had first laid eyes on the Deer Woman. A pull. A charge. A magnetic attraction so strong that it was all that she could do to not let her feet give way beneath her and allow herself to be dragged across the first-floor fiction area of the store by something invisible. Yet, this sort of inappropriately preposterous behaviour would certainly draw attention to her in the completely opposite manner to which she required. That is, if she was going to get up all close and personal to this intriguing woman.

She looked up and there she was. Mere metres away from her. It struck the Immortal Woman that the Deer Woman was rather fidgety. More so than usual. That she seemed to be wandering around in circles, not resting for any length of time on any book or section in that area. It was an uneasy sight to behold. It was as if she was high, jittery with the experience of finding oneself on edge with no idea what would soothe one's soul. Sure, bookstores normally have that ability. It's a part of their medicine. But it was clear that this was not the case for this woman today.

The Deer Woman was loitering, or rather wobbling, around the Junji Ito stand. His books, all grotesquely wide-eyed, melting nightmares, seemingly finding an echo in the Deer Woman's inner world lately, filled and fuelled by patterings of paranoia, and the utterly bizarre, seeping like wet ink, blotting and spreading into her ordinary everyday life. The Immortal Woman knew a little of such Japanese masters of horror. Indeed, somewhere in her memories was a whole lifetime of such stories. Though whether these were hers, or the lingering memories of a group of Japanese tourists she'd chosen, curiously, to brush up against on one of her London Tube rides, she couldn't be sure. It was one of those impulsive decisions, spawned out of boredom mixed with the taste for a world far removed from the one she inhabited daily, that she chose to only brush up against Japanese people for the whole weekend. The results being a certain confusion, a hunger for Konbini snacks from the 7-Eleven convenience store across the road from home, and a longing to wander through the quiet temple garden in Kyoto at the moon-viewing festival known as Tsukimi. Tears filled up in her eyes as she felt the deep aching nostalgia of sitting with grandparents whilst watching Enka singers on New Year's Eve whilst playing with Ultraman.

She was also prone to peculiar nightmares for the whole week after that particular weekend. Images of sneaking into too crowded izakaya filled with sweaty suited businessmen made her wake up feeling anxious, whilst visits from the urban legend slit-mouthed woman, Kuchisake-onna - and other strange creatures, crawling out of wells and television sets, half myth, half familiar from those horror remakes so popular over the last few decades - permeated her dreaming time.

The effect was so brutal and disturbing that she had chosen never to focus purely on one type of life force from then on, preferring a pick and mix instead. However, the deep-boned memories of being Japanese remained within her.

It was suddenly very useful now.

Have you read this one? It's ridiculously disturbing, but his imagination is extraordinary. If you like his other work, you'll like this one too.

She handed Ito's latest book to the Deer Woman with a smile.

The Deer Woman took it without saying anything. Truth be told this gesture had snapped her out of the spiral she was helter-skeltering down in her mind. For a moment she had a brief window of clarity. She sighed.

Oh, I'm sorry. I didn't mean to interrupt you. The Immortal Woman taking the sigh as an affront. She bowed a little - most likely influenced by the Japanese in her - and started to turn away.

Erm. No. Thank you. I love getting book recommendations. That's very kind of you.

The Deer Woman smiled at her. A shy, cautious, smile.

I've actually never read any of his books, but I do love the illustrations. Are you a manga fan? She looked the Immortal Woman up and down as she said that, not finding where tweed overlapped with anime. A strange combination indeed.

I am nowadays, yes. I worked on an exhibition of Japanese art for the museum that I work at a few years back. I guess my research opened me up to a whole new world.

Oh wow. What was the exhibition about?

The Deer Woman was genuinely interested. If for nothing more than a respite from her mind and the itchiness of her scalp. She tried hard to keep focusing on this odd, yet handsome looking woman, with an interest in Japan. Odd, for she did not seem as if she fitted into her surroundings in a manner that the Deer Woman could not quite say why exactly. And handsome, for there was no doubt that she was, with her smooth and flawless skin, wide intense eyes and jet-black silky hair that tumbled and tussled over her shoulders and down her back like a character from one of the books before them. It was hard to know how old she was, that's for sure.

It was on Shunga, erotic Japanese art. Have you heard of it? Really beautiful and quite shocking too!

The Deer Woman shook her head, but kept her gaze locked into the Immortal Woman's eyes. There was something familiar about her, but she couldn't quite put her finger on what it was. Still, she was harmless enough. Which, now that she'd thought that, struck the Deer Woman as a strange thing to think, and made her start to fidget even more, her toes curling and scrunching in her shoes, her feet awkwardly shifting from one to the other, as if her body knew something that her mind did not know. She could feel the hairs on her skin prick up, yet whether that was out of intrigue or fear she wasn't so certain - yet there was certainly a charge between them, that was for sure.

You say it's a museum where you work at? Here? In Manchester?

Yes. The Manchester Museum.

Aaaah. The Deer Woman felt a little uneasy as she heard these words. And yet, it was simply a coincidence that she worked there, wasn't it? Until the other month, she was a frequent visitor herself and often looked to this museum for inspiration. Aside from the fact that this happened to be the place where she had that little incident with the rusty nail, the museum had also been a place that had met her desire for a certain type of intimacy. One that even thinking of it now, was causing her to blush.

You see there had been more than one occasion whereby she had felt herself responding viscerally to what she was seeing in the museum. In the cool, low-lit interior, with its grand high ceilings, hushed corridors, and brooding, panelled cabinets, evocative of those devotional places where you'd go to pray, to reveal, to confess, she would find her breath quickening, her heart beating loudly - or so it seemed in the intimate silence - and her face would burn with a hot flush. She had lingered longer at each display of that visiting exhibition on feathers and wings, and at that other exhibition with those cases of sharp arrowheads. She had stood, transfixed, her mind racing with images she quickly shook away just in case someone could see the hot-limbed scenes that filled inside of her head, at the exhibition with that Austrian guy who preserved people's dead bodies, before stripping them of their flesh and hanging them in various poses. She'd become engrossed in this strange and eerie man and had ended up staying up late one evening to watch on TV a documentary crew following him around as he attempted to recreate the crucifixion, but using a real human's nervous system. It was both beautiful and macabre. And she loved it.

It was these oddities and peculiarities that made her feel turned-on as she would walk around the stately museum with its dark wood, dark musty smell, and dark bottles of dark secrets. Her breath would hasten, and she would find her senses become heightened, attuning to each and every creak that the museum would be expelling from its walls. There had been more than one occasion whereby she had fled to the bathroom to lock herself into one of the cubicles, pull up her dress, put her hand inside of her knickers, and pleasure herself, overcome by it all. She wouldn't take long. After flushing the toilet, she would wash her hands and splash water on her face and smile broadly at her reflection in the mirror.

You could say that this museum was both a place she courted as well as a place that courted her.

Of course, this woman standing before her, would never know this was a particular pastime she had frequently indulged in.

The more she looked, the more she was taken in by the sheer arresting unique beauty of her. She hadn't noticed before, but the Immortal Woman had the most astonishing green eyes, full lips and a presence that one could describe as a certain grandiosity. She was intrigued. Thinking about it, no wonder she worked at the museum. She probably fitted right in.

I love that museum.

The Immortal Woman had to bite her tongue to stop herself from letting on that she knew. And to stop herself from revealing that she also actually knew an awful lot about the Deer Woman's activities and places she frequented, due to her obsessive stalking. She didn't say anything, just nodded.

I have this...thing... about curiosities, you know. I've always had it. A fascination, I guess. I like to draw them, or take photos, or mainly just appreciate them. I'm sorry. You don't need to hear me blathering on. Thank you for the book recommendation. She still had the book in her hand and had already decided she was going to buy it.

Oh no. Not at all. You're a kindred soul, I can tell. I love all of that stuff too. Otherwise, I wouldn't be so passionate about my job. It certainly helps! She laughed and gave a huge, what she hoped was, friendly smile, towards the Deer Woman.

Look. This might seem like the strangest thing, and I know that we don't know each other, but it's really great to meet you, and so I was wondering whether you might fancy hanging out or going for a coffee sometime...erm...well that would be great. She was going to suggest meeting at the Museum gallery cafe but thought better of it considering the Deer Woman hadn't returned since the incident. Before the Deer Woman could answer, the Immortal Woman introduced herself.

I don't know about you but, it's bloody hard to meet new people these days don't you find? I'm not a drinker so I don't tend to go to bars or such places. I hope I'm not being too forward. It's just that it would be lovely to continue our conversation about weird things. Well, I think it would be.

She looked down at the floor, as if embarrassed by such an ask. Which, obviously, she really wasn't.

Of course, the only busy place that the Immortal Woman enjoyed was the London Tube, and the first day of sales at Harrods in London's fancy Kensington area.

She had discovered a long time ago that mixing alcohol and the taking of a life force did not match well together whatsoever. She always felt groggy the next day. Worse if the person she'd imbibed life from had had more than their fair share of imbibing themselves. Also, as people all over the world know, one's judgement and discernment tend to get blurred after a few drinks and her refined tendencies were often appalled by her previous night's tastes on more than one occasion. She may have been a wonderful whore once upon a time, but that was in Paris in the twenties, and her clients were the wealthiest of the wealthy then. Not the dregs of Manchester's night scene, especially down Deansgate Locks that's for sure. She shuddered at the memories and was taken out of spiralling down regret alley by the Deer Woman.

Sure. I can take your number. She handed the Immortal Woman her phone and the Immortal Woman was careful not to let their fingers touch. She figured that a cautious, give me your number, was better than a straight out no thanks.

Handing the phone back, as equally as carefully, they said their goodbyes. For now.

4.

Becoming.

One day at a time the Deer Woman started to change. In the beginning it began as a simple, yet annoying headache, and she would find herself scratching, absentmindedly, at the two places on her scalp, in line with the arch of her brows, where it was to become apparent, first to her, and over time to others, that she was morphing into something else. These two places on her head itched, and she scratched sometimes in her sleep and at other times out in public places such as at the library where she worked and where it was expected that you kept silence in all actions as an example to others. She would scratch and itch in the local Sainsbury's supermarket whilst contemplating which vegetables to buy for her dinner, which was not surprisingly rather off-putting for her fellow shoppers, and she would scratch and itch at the movies where frustrated cinema goers seated around and close to her, could be heard muttering and whispering and audibly sighing in annoyance, disgust, and disapproval.

She would also scratch and itch on her date night with her relatively new beau; whom she'd met a few weeks ago on Tinder, upon feeling that maybe the oddness she was feeling was due to not having gotten laid for a while. It quickly became obvious that sex and scratching were not the most compatible boudoir companions, and he did little to hide his revulsion whilst they were intimately entwined, with her fingers fondling and itching her scalp in time to his rhythm. And though it seemed that he tolerated this unusual combination for a time, it was unsurprising that gradually she stopped hearing from him, which, to be fair, wasn't a huge loss to her as their consummations didn't offer any help to ease the inconvenience. Besides, he didn't satisfy her increasingly lustful cravings.

Whether she was alarmed or not when first her hair fell away at these identical places on either side of her head, it was difficult to know. She took to wearing hats, jaunty and otherwise. Something was happening to her, slowly and carefully weaving its way through her, wanting out. When she awoke one morning and felt those places on her scalp had grown protrusions, she was concerned, at first that is, and then curious. She hid them well for a time, hats and headscarves and unusual hairdos that no one blinked nor winked at nor took a second glance. She resorted to revisiting that 90s hairdo she'd had during her clubbing years, the one that looked like Princess Leia in Star Wars: A New Hope, her hair swirled up in cute little side buns that for now managed to hide these unusual growths. You see she was odd like that, used to side glances and suspicious whispers. It was her nature you see, her wild nature, that no matter how many a tightly prim and posh wool pencil skirt she wriggled into from Next, nor how tidy of paperclips her desk was, she could never be tamed. Well now she had no chance of appearing to be a 'normal' member of society. Interestingly this made her sigh with relief and feel a beautiful calmness seep through her blood as if in agreement of her fate.

For a small window of time, she could still go out and assume and resume those social events that she so enjoyed. Such as a midwinter party over at Chorlton Eeves, complete with a firepit, mushrooms, both the magical and the 'on toast' varieties, fluorescent glow-in-the-dark body paint, which she chose to let herself be painted with from her waist upwards so that her nipples stuck out with the cold night air in twirls of red and white stripes like candy from Willy Wonka's factory. There they all were, a sprinkling of the local hippies, those brave and bold enough to be outside in the woods at that time of the year, dancing with cacao, the drug of choice for this particular burb of Manchester, painted up, tits and arses out, flinging themselves around in the dark to techno tunes and, for a time, live drummers, bare foot on the earth. They were wearing those headphones that, when removed momentarily, all senses fell back into the night's silent embrace, bar the sounds of the crunch of twigs and crisped leaves underfoot. Glancing around in the shadowed light, all one's gaze found were the shapes of silhouetted people moving between the trees, as if human and tree became the same, dancing alive, for just a brief moment in time.

After that small window closed, she took to dancing more in her flat. Sometimes she danced nude in her bedroom, but it wasn't quite the same, and she'd looked over and out the window once - she lived on the fifth floor of a city centre apartment block - and saw a couple peering over at her from the top of the NCP car park opposite, and she had ducked and crawled along the floor, cursing the fact that she could be overlooked in her own home. And yet when she returned, robed, she found the woman bent forwards and the man fucking her from behind. They were very well dressed, she'd noticed. As if they'd just been to an event, or the opera. She poured herself a sherry and settled in to watch their show. She'd pondered whether there was a whole subculture of city habituating people who constantly entertained each other through their windows, like peep shows for the vertical living. A VIP member only club of their own private salon of sensual treats.

The real difficulties began when the horns, and there was really no denying the fact that that's what they were becoming, started to protrude further, pushing off her hats, rudely and crudely poking their way through, nosey to see what was going on. They seemed to be pushing up roots, from some place deep in her head, as if her skull was the earth, a bone ancient and solid, desert parched, seemingly impossible, and yet they continued to grow. As they say, life always finds a way through, no matter the inconvenient circumstances.

She found that sleep was only possible and achievable if she lay on her back staring upwards towards the plastered white ceiling, but after a while that too proved a ridiculous and defunct possibility. So, she made a plush cushioned pillow and sitting, she would learn to snooze and doze when she needed to.

At around the same time she was surprised to find herself easily startled by the most innocuous sounds, the gentlest of noises and the most pastel of hues, and the lines and the shapes and the edges of the inner city that housed a thousand and one human-folk filled nights no longer made any logical or rational sense. She continued to bravely, and some might say foolishly, walk the city streets, now an unfamiliar and startling warren of suits and wheels and buses and littered fried chicken, the latter she found herself on more than one occasion crouching on her hinds sniffing and grunting at, whilst pigeons stared at her with blank one-eyed wonder. She found that the place she had once scorned became the sanctuary she felt safe to be this odd, chicken sniffing, pigeon-loving, startled being that she was becoming. Piccadilly Gardens, the home to those who spoke to the invisible, and those who called its green patches their address, became the only place in the city where she felt she could relax. Which was ironic really. Amongst the day dreamers and night pacers lying on benches and the old women feeding seed to the birds like some sort of demented version from Mary Poppins. The youth high on whatever the drug of choice was for that season. The pick and mix of sights unseen that seemed to be drawn to these gardens that don't really look like gardens. She'd recently read that this was once the site of the original Manchester Infirmary. Perhaps the cries of pain and anguish had fallen into the sodden earth through the guttering and drainage system of old, feeding the ground with tears, and prayers, and the gibbering of the morphine drugged patients.

And the horns continued to grow. They grew like branches, curling this way and that, jutting out of her rutting head. Gazing at them incredulously one day in the mirror she was struck and seized by the grip of beauty and awe she saw, turning her head this way and that way, admiring this uncanny work of art that was emanating life and exploration from her own scalp.

Moving through doorways became an art and others would wait patiently whilst she navigated herself magnificently. China shops and those with delicate items she no longer could frequent, which was a shame as she had a fondness for collecting traditional English teacups and pots from the Oxfam on Oldham Street.

Jumpers that would normally have been pulled over her head without a second thought, lay in a torn, forlorn, and ripped pile in the corner of her room, which was annoying particularly as this was after all the season of cashmere. Now, all of these were ruined. Luckily, she sought these out every year at the M&S outlet across town, so they weren't as pricey as purchasing them from the big M&S. But still. She had to take to robing herself in garments that buttoned down or else were generous with their zips or wrap.

And she was obviously garnering plenty of attention as she manoeuvred around the city during her daily affairs. From the frank glances and stares of other shoppers to the pointing with chubby fingers of children, it was now impossible to hide what was happening to her body. She didn't mind these wordless judgments, yet it was when the scallies, around her now beloved Piccadilly Gardens, began to make comments as she walked through, that she felt the weight of being different on her shoulders. She recalled how many years ago; after travelling to India for six months, she'd arrived home with a penchant for wearing bindis every day. A pretty little sparkling jewel of colour in the centre of her brow. To be fair, she wasn't alone in this aesthetic decorating, as proven by all the festivals she attended in the mid-90s - it was all the rage at the time. But it was one day, walking around W. H. Smiths, that some scally came up to her and shouted *what the fuck 'ave ya got on ya forehead mate!??* to her, pointing aggressively at her face, and, having momentarily forgotten that she was wearing a bindi that day, took her by surprise and caused her to put down the jigsaw puzzle of a country house and cats that she was purchasing for a friend's birthday, and hurry out of the store. The people of Manchester are not necessarily au fait with someone with horns poking out of their head. Now, if she was in Brighton, that could have been a very different story. But she wasn't. This was her home. She liked the grit of this Northern city.

The final straw came when she realised that feigning fighting flu, and abject weariness, week after week, was not boding well with her colleagues and her work. Though working at a library was deliriously charming for a woman easily spooked by, well, everything, she was finding that she had to control the urge to chew upon the books themselves. They smelled good. Of trees and old lands. Startlingly, a longing lurked at her heart to ingest their flavours and stories, literally. Literal literary she thought, smiling. The smile fell fast as she realised that it might not be long before she was caught in an uncompromising position with Audubon's 'Birds of America', its wingspan pages torn, fluttering and spilling out of her mouth. No, she couldn't bear the idea of being found in such a manner, and so she hung up her archival aptitude and resigned post haste.

Feeling a flutter of fleeting fear now that she had lost her reasoning to stay relational and appropriate for such proper society without her work to focus on, the Deer Woman felt her legs were beginning to buckle, metaphorically so of course, beneath her. She was alone in this strange situation and, bar her own thoughts - and those were not the most reliable - she knew that she needed to seek solace and support in someone who would not turn her away, nor turn away from, such an oddity of a situation. So, with that in mind, and suspecting that she might know something that could address her affliction, in the first week in January of a brand-new year, she tentatively sent the Immortal Woman a text asking if she remembered her and whether she would still like to meet up.

Obviously, the answer to both of those questions was yes.

The following week they met up at Chapter One Books in the Northern Quarter, a sweet escapist cafe cum bookstore and other fabulous finery, frequented by shy local creatives and the odd passerby from out of town. The Deer Woman arrived first, ordered a rainbow sponge cake and a pot of Earl Grey tea. She positioned herself at a table by the window and was nervously pushing pieces of her cake around her plate, when the Immortal Woman showed up.

Hi

Hi

As is most usual in such situations where two strangers with a curiosity about the other meet up for the first time, there was a brief awkward exchange of pleasantries, about the weather, the cafe, the obligatory happy New Year greetings, and then silence.

The Deer Woman seemed more composed than the last time she had seen her, though whether that was simply due to her outfit, the Immortal Woman wasn't clear. The Deer Woman was attired in a satin blue and white kimono with long draped sleeves, white cowboy boots, and heavy blue eyeliner circling her wide, hazel, eyes. Adding to this already dramatic look was a huge, what looked like, statement art piece, mushrooming out from her head, swathed in silk scarves. She certainly stood out and for a brief moment, the Immortal Woman felt drab, her hands absentmindedly smoothing down her own prim, black woollen skirt, damning herself for not considering that perhaps this was more than just a coffee date. Despite the charge that she expected from the Deer Woman, she felt nervous. She shook her head just as the Deer Woman broke the silence.

Look. I know that this might sound strange. And it is. And no problem at all if you have no idea what I'm talking about. The Deer Woman laughed nervously, tossing her head back. *Do. Do you have any idea what is going on...with me. With my...head? I don't know why I'm asking you to be honest, but for some strange reason I think you might be able to...*

At this point, she stopped speaking and instead untied the elaborate headscarf that was wound around her head. She could feel the Immortal Woman's gaze taking in her newly unveiled, very obvious horns.

I... I...don't. But...

Sorry...

No. No wait. It's ok. Please. Talk to me. Please.

Look, I called you because I feel like I know you. That you understand. Which doesn't make any sense, does it? I mean, I don't even understand what's happening to me. I've not felt right since I ...since I had a little accident a few months back. At the museum. That you work at. And then meeting at the bookstore. I don't know, but it's too much of a coincidence. Or maybe I want it to be.

The Deer Woman blushed as she spoke these words, before remembering why she had invited the Immortal Woman for tea in the first place.

But this...this isn't normal, is it?

She pointed to her head.

Well. No. But... It's striking.

The Immortal Woman took a deep breath in.

It's really beautiful. And fuck normal, whatever the hell that is.

The Immortal Woman burst out laughing. Strangely she was having such a wonderful time. She felt intoxicated. And hopeful. No. No. Don't go there. No.

The Deer Woman sniggered. Then blushed once more. Seeming to visibly relax in her seat as if the whole time she had been waiting to breathe out, she burst out laughing too.

God, thank you. I mean. It really is so ridiculous, isn't it? I don't know. I feel different. And yet also, more of myself. I can't explain it.

For a brief moment she disappeared somewhere, her gaze drifting away and into a place no one else could glimpse. The Immortal Woman sat patiently, biding her time, bewitched and bewildered. When she came to, the Deer Woman's face had changed. Fear now replaced the regal calm that only moments ago had transfixed the other woman. She leaned in towards the Immortal Woman, placing her hand on her leg. The Immortal Woman glanced down at the hand on her thigh and stiffened. *It's ok,* she thought. *I'm ok.*

Can you help me? The Deer Woman's whisper had an edge to it. A desperate edge. It was a plea.

The Immortal Woman shook her head slowly. *Let me see what I can find out. These weird things are happening more and more these days. It's almost like the world has come off its axis or...something. Don't you think?*

She didn't know what else to say. How could she reveal to the Deer Woman that she had a hunch that somehow their fates were entwined. She didn't fully comprehend it herself.

Almost as quickly as it had appeared, the Deer Woman's expression changed again and she relaxed back, stabbing at a piece of cake on her plate before popping it into her mouth. A soft smile spread across her face.

It's strange but, in some ways this all feels right. Yet obviously, having this, she pointed to her horns, *kind of breaks up your routine, you know. I feel like a minor celebrity wandering through town at times, I have to admit. People are rather blatant with their open mouths and blank stares. No one's asked for my autograph yet though.*

Both women started to laugh again. Loud. Giddy. Raucous. A few glances from the shy ones around them and they started to whisper.

The Deer Woman, though disappointed and slightly irritated that the other woman wasn't more forthcoming in her information – for she was certain that she knew more than she was letting on - found the Immortal Woman to be rather interesting in a not so unpleasant way. She wondered about her background, where she was from, *can't be from around here, too unusual looking to be local* she thought. She noticed how reserved she seemed, coy, refusing a hug, or a handshake upon meeting. And yet, how familiar she was with her too. She was interested. Curious. A paradox. The Deer Woman found that strangely arousing, especially when she added in a fantasy that the Immortal Woman was repulsed by her horns. Yet she knew that wasn't the case. Clearly. She could feel this woman's lust and desire. It emanated from her with such a heat that the Deer Woman had to roll up her giant kimono sleeves in order to cool down. The revealing of her naked arms sent the Immortal Woman into more of a lustful revelry, her glances now taking in the shape of their gentle yet firm curves. How she ached to touch the skin, this flesh proffered before her, however she knew that was unwise.

They decided to continue their under the table flirtations somewhere more grown-up, and settled upon Flok, a corner establishment on Stephenson Square, a small bar with wooden booths and a hard liquor vibe. They were the only punters in the place upon their arrival, and if any more arrived later, the women were oblivious.

White wine for one woman, soda water for the other, they sat and drank and avoided touching and laughed long after the day turned over into night. They spoke about the strange occurrences that were happening in their city lately, their mutual adoration of nature and animals. One drink, then two, then one more for the road.

And then the Immortal Woman mentioned the Harpist.

The Harpist was a local legend. Well. She was an international legend to be fair. But it was rumoured that she lived in Manchester, though no one seemed to know exactly where she abided. Carefully and curiously, the Immortal Woman mentioned that she had two tickets to go see her live the following weekend at the Bridgewater Hall, and hedging her bets, she invited the Deer Woman to be her plus one. Delighted, the Deer Woman said yes. She'd heard strange rumours about this Harpist and her music but had never imagined that she would ever get to see her. What a treat! Especially as it was pretty impossible to get tickets. You had to be invited personally from someone who had connections, and the Deer Woman did not know, nor tended to hang out with or near, any such persons of such high star-status pedigree.

Fuck it! Why not? As long as they had seats to the side, so she wouldn't be inadvertently blocking anyone else's view with her horns, she figured it would be fun. In answer to the question of how she had gotten hold of these tickets, the Immortal Woman simply shrugged and said that she had contacts. She winked as she said this.

Whatever was going on the Deer Woman had no idea of, but it didn't matter. She was enjoying the feel of this woman's desire. She could smell it now. It had a scent of a dark and dirty nightclub, one from the late 80s with the occasional suggestion of poppers. It was the scent of sweat and leather and for some reason this made the Deer Woman's leg begin to quiver. But most of all, she could sense something about her. Something feral. As if she too was not what she seemed. Maybe none of us are, the Deer Woman wondered on the way home after their six hour hang out.

She felt tipsy, delirious and in a kind of bemusing way, her legs bowed from beneath her several times as she walked. To anyone who crossed her path that evening, she looked like a dancer, her gait, though unsure, seemed impossibly graceful, as she ambled down the streets. Upon occasion her feet would cross, and she would stumble ungainly letting out a laugh that sounded more akin to a wild bark. To those she passed by, she looked inebriated, a not so uncommon sight in the city centre.

5.

Vials full of tears and wax.

They had the most perfect seats three rows back from the stage, and to the side, exactly as the Deer Woman had gently requested. As they took their seats, she could feel the buzz of excitement as their fellow audience members fussed to find theirs and position themselves as comfortably as possible. Everyone was dressed up, and the Deer Woman's gaze caught the reflections from sequins and diamonds, the grease of pomade slicked hair, and the shine in the darting eyes of her fellow audience attendees.

As she took it all in, and as each seat was filled, the Deer Woman recalled the many rumours that abounded about the Harpist. They were both plentiful and preposterous.

Such as, she was rumoured to have had an affair with the senator of Delaware. That she used to be a madam in a brothel in the Nevada desert. That she convened with the CIA to capture the famous diamond thief, Smith McDonald, using her concert to trap him in the audience. That she used to fly jets for the country back in the Second World War, which of course, seemed the most ludicrous of them all because that would mean she was close to a hundred years old, surely? That she was a hairdresser to Minna Sarrow, a witch and the (supposed) cause of the terrible affliction of the ten plagues upon the county of Hertfordshire in the late 80s - because someone wrote a terrible review in the Yellow Pages about her hairdressing abilities.

The stories were endless, looping from the famous to the fantastical and landing in the firm understanding that perhaps it was impossible to really know the truth about her.

The Harpist.

The one that people came to see. Playing her harp. Causing grown men to break down, lovers to confess their sins, old grievances that had lasted decades to dissolve in a puff of dandelion seeds. The Harpist and her music touched their hearts in ways that only a Beloved could know. The kind of Beloved that had nestled its way into all the lonely nooks and crannies of the places where the heart hadn't been seen or felt for so long. Maybe, not ever.

Her music made people youthful again. Carefree. Like children. Absorbed in enchantment for what seemed like eternity, as if time was simply a myth and a misunderstanding. As the Harpist's music boastfully swelled and became bashful once more, so too did time, expanding and contracting like a cosmic accordion.

As the Harpist often commented to her public during those evenings, why on earth should she have to work eight hours a day if one hour and forty minutes was all it took to propel people to the stars and back again.

And the audience would laugh. And cry. Mainly cry.

And it was all because of the strings that the Harpist played. The strings that no one knew what they were made of or where they were from. Impossible strings, unbreakable, stronger than the most brutish of forces, their resonance an exquisite sound like nothing else ever heard.

Not that it mattered to them. But for her it was the secret to everything. For the strings came, not from catgut, nor wire, but from the bodies of certain people. Well, their hearts, to be exact. A human heart, each string drawn out, strand by strand.

She would read the obituaries. She knew exactly the day where the most glorious of lives were noted. Which papers to find them in. Usually it was in those broadsheets which no one really read, just held open and displayed one's preference for cheese and port and gout whilst the pages hid rotund stomachs, trapped gas, and pompous ass behaviour.

The Harpist would wait in cafes in Didsbury, on a Sunday late afternoon, smoking a cigarette, lurking behind dark glasses and a coffee that was never fully sipped, going cold, gathering dust particles, which she didn't seem to mind, not giving any care or glance to. She waited for them to finish their afternoon tea out with their wife and two small kids with jam around their faces, on their hands, stickiness making her wince. The wife always looked pained, as if her lips were stapled shut, her husband hiding behind the pages of the paper, not reading any words to be sure, probably snoozing, ignoring this chaos of family, and hearts, and children, counting down, nay, wasting the hours before he could get back to the office Monday early morning. Steel and greys and clocks and glass desks and appointments and that secretary with the peachy round ass in her tight black skirt and the way she smiled at his every behest.

Once they had left, the Harpist would get up immediately and sweep the paper like a crow that had had its beady eye on its treasure all along, and leave. She'd grab a black cab and sit wordlessly as life through Rusholme passed her by. She wondered when so many of the shops had become those places to smoke shisha pipes. She tried to remember what it was like before. So many Indian restaurants. They had often joked, her and her sister, that there was probably one massive kitchen that ran all the way down this part of the city, passing palak paneer and garlic naans up and down like ants. The food was mostly filling, so your belly bowled in bloat, the taste of undisclosed spice lingering before you as you breathed out in the cooler night air.

She got the bus to stop just past the Museum and hurried down the road away from it.

Once home she would find the pages where dead people's lives were summarised in neat paragraphs of a word count never exceeding two hundred, unless they were very important people indeed. Their bodies would still be warm. Their hearts would still remember. Their passing away may be still only fresh to the tear-stained cheeks of their loved ones, but their bodies were not yet laid to rest or finished in their service to the world. The world of music that is.

For that was the key. The strings did not work if the heart hadn't belonged to someone who knew how to love. Who had risked opening up so violently vulnerable to another. Who was filled with the swell and tell of generosity and care, so careful so as not to break the other's own heart. Their heart, still so full that it's a wonder that it hadn't split and burst and spilled its swollen unspent adoration when laid to rest.

They had to have felt love so deeply that it had imprinted itself onto their heart. So embedded and embodied that if you knew where to look, like she did, you could see the indentations, the heartaches, the pain, the yearnings, morse-coded onto its memory.

Her favourites were the hearts of those who had had long and happy marriages or love stories that endured the test of its pages. Sure, happiness is subjective, she's no idealist. Nor dreamer. You couldn't be in an occupation such as hers with a head only knowing imagined clouds. But a heart that had settled into a love with such comfort, with such a known sense of it, tended to ripen the heart. To toughen it up in its complacency. It had a nobility to it.

A resilience. It was sure of itself in a way, puffed up and proud. But homely too. Quiet. Steady. Sure. Cosy. You could trust a heart like that. You could feel it in the palm of your hand. Literally. It held a certain gravitas that was always a joy to feel.

It always felt like it carried the weight of a million memories. You could sense them there. Silent now. Yet not forgotten. Imprinted forever on the muscled flesh. She always got excited then, her own heart would beat faster, her palms sweat. She would have to carefully place the heart down upon the silver metal tray whilst she composed herself. For the thing was, if she could catch a glimmer of the songs this heart knew how to sing just from holding the meat in her hand, then she could not even imagine what music it would play and offer and lament and rejoice when plucked. She licked her lips at the thought. Her heart still beating fast. Steadying her hand and her mind, she continued her work. This is where the skill lies. Even before it was offered to the public's gaze and ears, this was the most important step of them all.

The skill lay in separating the ligaments from everything else. You needed a magnifying glass that facing the wrong way would terrify whatever might be hiding within the dark recesses of your facial pores; a scalpel that was so sharp that it could sever your own

Harpist's dressing room, stowed with the rest of her possessions for that evening and taken home with her, where the chest was placed on the dressing table in the room where she kept her precious instrument.

Now this was all well and good, and though these vials of tears would be counted and annotated for the Harpist's records - for if one was found to be unusually effective, then it was always worth keeping one eye on the comings, and particularly the goings, of that family name - unfortunately, upon occasion, mistakes were made and the numbers miscalculated. Though fortunately, that is, for the Immortal Woman, as she'd managed to thieve the bottle of tears that the Deer Woman had joyously and movingly spilled into the vial from the Harpist's performance, without anyone noticing, and she felt giddy, like a young woman, at her achievement.

It was the Maestro who had shown the Harpist the human heartstring of a lover, by exposing the one that he kept in a pouch around his neck. It was a string strung from the heart of his dead wife. They had been married for thirty-seven years, she was the mother of their five children, all grown up now, flown the nest, scattered across the seas. His beloved wife had died in his arms, her illness terminal, very sad, so sad, everyone said. He hadn't explained how he had her heart, if she veered towards curiosity in the matter he would shoo her question away in annoyance. He thought he would make strings for his bow out of it, and play his beloved violin, but each time that he placed the bow carefully against the violin strings, each bow heart hair would snap and furl away from his touch, burning and singed and sad too. But he had kept the bow, with its broken strings echoing his broken heart, and would stroke it at night in bed with himself alone and longing for her touch. His presence was soothed by the heartstring of her absence.

Before he died, he had called to the Harpist and told her that there was something that she had to do, needed to do, begged her to do, if she loved him at all. And she did love him. He had created her, stretched, and teased her like any of his instruments and for that reason she would do anything he asked of her, especially his dying wishes. She wasn't surprised when he required of her to make a heartstring from his own heart, which had known love, the love of his wife and the love of music and make a new harp for herself to play.

A week after he was publicly buried and privately mourned, a box arrived at her home with his heart in it. Disgusted at first, she read the instructions that he had written in his spidery handwriting, all shaken whilst his own heart was simultaneously being shaken by death's stranglehold on him. It was the first heart that she had taken from. But not the last.

Over the years of course she had tried many different heartstrings from many different hearts. She hadn't been so discerning at first and hadn't known how differently each heart would sound. The young hearts, though easier to peel away the ligaments that she needed, were crude and unlived, their sound more suited to a kindergarten classroom's singsong. The hearts of the lonely sounded bitter and full of regret, their sound echoing like melancholy and discordant. They made her nose turn up in repulsion.

The rich men's hearts sounded glorious and jolly yet lacking in subtlety and nuance. Their sound was, quite frankly, boring.

The hearts of the unkempt and unwashed, those bodies that were easier to source from, had the sort of sound that clung to your own skin for days. Grasping and pleading and needy.

The heartstrings of the intelligent, though perfectly in tune and undoubtedly clever, lacked soul, lacked substance, the notes hanging empty in the air.

No. It was the heartstrings from lovers that made for the best notes. Those that held their aching and yearning, akin to the stirrings of angels singing, that made you blush for no reason. Those that caused the listener to pine for their first love, to recall hot flesh on hot nights, to remember the tangibility of curves, scents, touch and the whispers that only lovers knew the language to. These were the sounds of heartaches and heartbreaks and I do's and forever. The sounds would linger, slip down your throat, kiss the back of your neck, and squeeze you tight in your bed at night. These were the sounds that made you throb and wet and moan. These were the sounds of tenderness, weeping and goodbyes.

And the tears were needed. Each string needed to be fed, their thirst unrivalled and unmatched. No ordinary water would suffice. No special oils. The strings would discard and reject these with impudence and a certain arrogance. No. They needed real tears from those whose hearts understood. And so, after each performance when she was alone, she would bathe them, like a lover herself, which she was. She would sing to them, rub her naked flesh against them. Breathe her secret longings to them. Shower them with gifts of praise and adoration. Salute herself to their beauty. Weep at her own solitude and loneliness, knowing that her heart would never, could never, be one of them.

Inside the other glass vial beneath the seat of the listener, alongside the vial for one's tears, was a miniature silver spoon, akin to those found in salubrious parlours, low lit, velvet coated, with the haze of the hazy hanging in the air. The drug of choice, served on plates, each partaker handed a small spoon upon entrance. The powder brought to the nostrils, sniffed swiftly, its impact immediate, shifting the shape of the air, the ground changing form, one's identity moulded into whatever fancy the imagined realms decided. She knew of these places and thought of them fondly.

There were no such drugs available for consumption, or sniffing, during her performance. Good lord no. The silver spoons were for another use. A strange use. As she plucked the strings, the sounds found the ears of its audience, curling its way into their eardrums and straight to their pineal gland. The side-effect of this ear-gasm was wax. Lots and lots of wax. Ear wax leaked out like the golden drippings of a saint. The audience were instructed to collect this offering with the spoon and deposit it into the vial. This one they were instructed to leave on a small silver tray that lay under their seats.

Only the most special ear wax would be chosen. Sometimes there was none that befitted such an offering. The wax that did pass the mark she massaged into the flesh of her beloved, her harp. She would bring her body in close to her instrument, legs open, reaching as far as she could around the Walnut body of her harp, her head to the side, her eyes closed, lips slightly parted.

This was for her. Her private moment.

Backstage after the show, the thank yous, and it's my pleasure and I'm glad you enjoyed it, and smiles and words, sat in her dressing room, all was quiet. She loved this moment. The stillness. The moment after the last symphonic crescendo had died away. Just this. She sighs and reaches for her brandy.

Meanwhile, in the square outside of the Bridgewater Hall, the Immortal Woman was delighted by the evening's unfolding, and the special watery treasure she courted that lay waiting in her pocket. She was careful not to touch the Deer Woman as they said goodbye and thank you so much and that was incredible and the best show I've ever seen and air kisses and after she watched the Deer Woman's slight frame and odd gait disappear into the night, she returned home to the apartment that she shared with her sister. This was a series of unused rooms beneath the Royal Northern College of Music, and she waited excitedly for her sister's return from the concert. Once home, she showed her the vial with a smile on her face.

Her sister, the Harpist, smiled wanly back and then the Immortal Woman started to laugh so hysterically that if you were walking past the College at that exact moment you might have noticed an odd quiver from the building itself, and, unable to shake an unease that crept up your spine, you'd pull your collar up higher and scurry past.

The Immortal Woman was muttering.

It's different. Different. I feel it. It will set you, us free. I. I think I'm in love, sister. These tears. These. I thought to steal these, her tears, to give to you, for you, for us, my sister, because maybe these would keep the strings moist forever and you, sister, you could stop having to dig up bodies as it is surely getting tiresome and, but no, no. If this woman has the rejuvenation and regeneration powers of a deer like I suspect and no, I FEEL, I would be giving you, us, the ultimate gift and then maybe you, my sister could relax a little and rest and we could take a vacation and ...and....and....But no.

And just like that, the Immortal Woman's expression changed. Her eyes narrowed, her jaw tightened. And she took a step back from the Harpist.

They're mine. Mine. You can't have them. I need them. I need them.

She was clutching the vial now, close to her chest, her eyes narrowing. Gibbering away. Nonsense. Her eyes wild. Spittle flying out of her mouth.

The Harpist sighed, knowing these signs and wanting to shake her sister awake to the folly of it all. The folly of falling in love with someone and having their body so close yet impossible. She knows what happens. She's been there many times. Many, many times. It can't happen again. She can't return home from a tour or concert and be confronted with a desiccated body with a dead heart in Tupperware in the fridge, albeit a badly removed one. For sure, removing this muscle was not a skill the Immortal Woman possessed. Fragments of heart flesh still hanging from where an arrow had pierced it from when her sister had yet again proclaimed that this heart had held the most love of all.

It's not possible. She cannot help but kill these lovers with love itself. A cruel twisted irony for the one who can live forever.

Fuck their lives sometimes thinks the Harpist.

This could all have gone the same way but for three things. One, the Harpist had never had any desire, not an ounce, to use the heartstrings from an animal before. It was far too risky as one could never be really sure what the true nature of an animal's understanding and feeling of love would sound like. But a human with the kindred of a deer, that most magical of creatures, now that was intriguing.

Two, this utterance of love. What did it mean? The Harpist had seen her sister in love before, of course. But it was dangerous. This was dangerous. It couldn't end well for any of them. She was certain of that.

And three, because they do say that three is the magic number, is the fact that the Deer Woman disappeared a few weeks later.

6.

Rumours abound about where she is.

It was about now that she could smell it in the air, calling her, twitching her nostrils searching for a catch of its scent. A mystery, at first scant and faint and fleeting, particularly when engulfed daily by the fumes of noxious diesel, takeaways or perfumes, but it was there underneath it all. And soon the allure and seduction of the undeniable rich, moist, fertile forest became too strong a force to resist anymore. It pulled at the Deer Woman, tugged at the antennae on her head, almost as if her horns needed its feed and fauna, the verdant, lush, deep green, the floor of flowers, the songs of winged ones at dawn. And it was precisely at this hour, just at the pause before day, when all are sleeping in dreams, that she awoke, startlingly so, one day which happened to be the second day of February and knew that it was time. She could bear it no longer. A few hours later she had put her flat on the market. In a highly up and coming gentrified area, it sold within a week at the asking price. Her heart beat faster now, a trot, a gallop, an excited and expectant dance was clipping the bare soles of her feet against what seemed so odd and unnatural in its fibres; her carpeted living room floor. Her luscious and magnificent horns danced too with glee, and finally, letters to loved ones written by hand, all scrawled and posted with love, she fled.

Now, unsure as to what possessions, of a human kind, she might be needing on her travels, the Deer Woman chose to take with her only a few items. Three kimonos. Two head scarves. One pair of red Manolo Blahnik shoes that she had thrifted from a charity shop in Wilmslow several years ago but had never worn (which was even more unlikely now, but still). A book of poems by Emily Dickinson. A crimson velvet lipstick from Kiko's make-up store. Her back scratcher, which had become even more of an essential item for her over the last few months. And the cassette tape of her favourite 80s band, *The Necessities*. Whether it was simply her parents who feigned a certain sweet story, or whether there was truth to the fact, the Deer Woman had apparently, and allegedly, known all the words to the songs on their one and only album, despite never having heard them prior to her father purchasing the tape, when she was merely five years old. Even though her musical tastes had changed over the years, there was something sentimental about the tape, so she packed that item too.

First, she fled to Heaton Park. To be fair, she knew that this wasn't ideal. It wasn't a place she could relax and never be noticed. But she had always been drawn to that tree in the woods. The large oak with its inviting bough, a canopy for the lost and wounded. She'd seen this tree in each season, wearing its blossom, lush deep green foliage, bare branches, branches laden with snow. The ground littered with the brown leaves of its shedding. She trusted that tree. She had often sought shelter and respite there.

Save for the squirrels, she was alone that day. It was early and the tree was not on the usual runners' path. She hugged the tree, seeking the comfort that she'd received so many times before. This time though this just irritated her and before she knew it, she was scratching her head against the trunk, bark against horns, bucking. This felt amazingly satisfying to her and she continued for a while, completely forgetting anything else.

After some time, it was clear that this was not the place for her. She could hear the small yet resolute cries of children playing nearby; their shrieks, upsetting to her unsettled new nature. The parents calling to them, their steps upon the gravelly paths unnerving to her newly thin skin, interrupting her respite. She flinched and shook her head, feeling at odds with someone she used to be. That is, a human woman.

She headed to the animal corner. And straight to the alpacas. There were three of them, two white and one brown. They looked at her blinking with their big doll eyes. She blinked back, a slight panic arising in her as she realised that though she was not quite fully human anymore, she wasn't yet fully an animal either. They continued for a while, staring, blinking, until she left, suddenly realising where she needed to go.

It was obvious really. She needed to be around other deer, and the only place she could think to find that was at Dunham Massey. A Northern estate with olden oak and beech trees, stone outbuildings, a shop selling fancy local dairy ice-cream, and of course, deer.

The thing is, as one might well imagine, the deer were at first suspicious of, and then, perplexed by, the Deer Woman. She smelt like them. She acted like them. She even had antlers like theirs, delicate, twisting and branching out in the same graceful way. But she looked like one of those others. The humans that come and visit and try to get close and let their squirming, shouty kids storm towards them, and their dogs to come sniff and provoke them and pee on their patch. Truth be told, they weren't massively fond of the humans and though they knew that they were part of what attracted people to the estate, they had learned over the years how to hide from their vision and exist without the scrutinising, patronising, sometimes awed, stares from them. Also, because of their sensitive nature, the deer were easily startled most of the time. A single step on a twig ten metres away and it was as if someone had broken said twig right by their ear.

Not the best conversationalists to be fair. And, though she might be becoming feral and primal and of the earth, she still longed for intelligent conversation. Actually, and quite horrifyingly, she found the deer, albeit beautiful, graceful, and curious creatures, to be rather unstimulating. Simple, magical creatures that's for sure, whispering about new pathways and the codes that the earth was telling them through its pulses, but apart from this, they were mostly silent. Listening. Observing. Trying not to spook themselves to be fair.

And so, she fled again. This time she ran. And ran. And ran some more. She did so much running that it's impossible to tell you just how much running she did and just how far across the globe her little legs with her feet that felt like hooves, took her. Let's just say they took her a long way away from home.

Over time the rumours, which, like the wind which had carried her unceremoniously and unobtrusively to her fate, began to stir up their own little whirlwind, until a storm of telling and retelling fell over the lands and across the seas. Some, who had seen her, found themselves telling intimate loved ones, strangers and anyone who had a taste and mind for magic, what they had seen. And so, they, the people of the lands and across the seas, came to visit with her, where she resided, seated under the most grandiose oak tree in the centre of the forest, somewhere in Russia, resplendent and majestic in a red organza and satin floral-patterned dress. Some said that if you squinted at this said dress it would appear that it was itself alive, wriggling snakes, fluttering butterflies and crawling neon beetles running amok amongst vines and brambles.

She herself was most courteous and polite and would welcome with open arms and an open and generous heart any guest who had found their way through the thickets of her wonderland. She would invite them to choose a teacup, and it was a most curious thing that each one hung so delicately on her antlers which had grown to fullness by now. These teacups, the guests were to learn, were gifts from passing adventuring men and women, explorers of the natural world. In a kooky twist of fate, often bringing their wares, and found, and often stolen - she didn't judge - treasures, to take to reside in the most important museums across the globe, such as, the 'National Museum of Natural Curiosities', the 'Sacred Earth Objects Museum', and, one time she was surprised to hear, the 'Manchester Museum' where once upon a time an ordinary woman's story had begun. These adventuring men and women, dashingly handsome, majestically alluring, and foppishly polite, seemed always in want and need of a brewed pot of tea to be drunk with pointed pinkie fingers and a digestive biscuit or two, no matter the heroic adventure in which they would find themselves. They would sit close to her and tell tales of whence they came and where they were going, and they came with stories of lands with names and folklores and scents all new and delightful to her. She knew this because she could smell these layered aromas upon their skin when they moved in close for an invited kiss or frolic against the bark and grass.

She may have turned into something no longer quite human, something more wild than ever before, but she was still a woman. These travellers would tell others of her, and the word spread like the moss over lands and the waves across the seas.

Upon occasion an adventuring man or woman would fall immediately, deeply, and heart-achingly in love with her, and as she shook her head in decline of their offers of wooing and homemaking, smiling peacefully, they would ask if she ever did indeed, even for a fleeting moment, miss her old life. The smog and the frantic A to B pacing of the city. The unnatural imposed silence and musty scents of the library with its books all lined up with neat words like obedient soldiers. The queues - and the frozen peas for that matter - of fluorescent lit supermarkets. Or how about the concrete jungle beneath her feet, or the closed four walls that used to house her in solitude, and often loneliness, each and every night. She shook her head. No. Absolutely not. And these amorous and heart-broken guests would find themselves having to shake off their own laments, which would creep upon them like vines, of living in a world sometimes far too complex and civilised for some part of their knowing.

She would offer fine cakes and pastries and share stories. The birds especially loved to listen, and they too would find a space and place for their perch, their song held for now, only an occasional trill ringing out in agreeance and delight. You see, the forest had tales to tell her. The trees and the leaves, the fauna and flora, the foxes and wild cats. Just as she had once ached and hungered for, she was now able to converse with these animals she had only admired from behind glass. This made her very content and joyful indeed.

The others would sit and drink their tea and eat their cake, the crumbs gobbled rapidly by the little creatures that had joined them. They would listen enraptured and enchanted and go home full, not just of belly, but of remembering and of her. Her, in her fabulous frock, with the deer horns growing out of her head.

Now, this was all very well and good and enchanting and obviously, unsustainable. That's the problem with so many of these tales; they never let you poke your nose into what happens further down the line. Sadly, for most, happily ever after is simply one for the storybooks. And so it was, that finding the winds of restlessness blowing on her as the time rolled on, she decided to go home, or at least some semblance of home, and make her way back to Manchester.

Alderley Edge to be precise. A place notorious for nefarious activities of witchcraft and magic. Or so it was said. But she had always enjoyed walking through the woods when she was only a human; crafting rituals on a full moon or over Halloween with her sister; and she had felt an uncanny fondness for the woods that were nestled beside the village that was a favoured home for all manner of rich footballers and fancy folk.

Which is just as well. Because everything took a strange turn one day, unfortunately for the Deer Woman. But of good fortune for destiny to unfold itself, and for this tale to tell its more.

7.

The secret to regeneration.

The Immortal Woman's obsession with
Woman over the last fourteen months, ha
into something unpleasant. Well, even m
unpleasant than usual. She'd lost control
and had taken to riding the night buses th
and down Oxford Road, mainly carrying s
drunks. Usually, one and the same. She
fussy. Her hunger was now more for feed
ghost that could never be satiated, rathe
tasteful foray into an immortal banquet.
care. If the Deer Woman had disappear
trace, then what chance did she have o
herself. She was tired. She got careless
And she looked insane quite frankly. He
composed composure crumbling at th
was losing her grip on the act, so tireso
demanding, of maintaining her sanity'

She'd also taken to dabbing a teeny tiny drop of he Deer Woman's tears onto her neck every day upon vaking up, believing that this act of perfuming herself vith the Deer Woman's tears would give her the neans to commune with her as the seasons passed. he wondered whether her antlers had shed as the eaves had turned brown and gold and orange once nore. Of course, the tears gave up no answers to her uestions. Obviously.

Her sister had had enough. Watching the nmortal Woman's undoing was having an impact on oth of their lives.

The Harpist was the older sister and so it had fallen to her to take care of her little sister. They re both old. Older than they appeared. Much older an they appeared. Their magic kept death away and they were death's mistresses both. It was a cruel p. They both fed upon hearts and life beats and mories and the feelings and emotions of others.

Though their story may certainly sound strange, to r ears and mine, there have been stranger tales l, and stranger stories will yet be borne.

Their story was the result of a young girl's over ve imagination. A girl who lived in a village, a long, time ago, by a stream that swished and swirled

and told her stories to keep her heart warm and for company. For the girl was an orphan and her only other friend, besides the stream, was a bear. The bear was kind and generous, but despite these qualities, he was still a beastly bear - big and furry and with sharp teeth and a cry that made your hair blow. And so, in order to support the little girl - for he, as a bear, did not need anything from the human world - he would dress up with bells on his feet, carry a small cassette machine to the local markets, play music and dance for money. Though some may scoff at such behaviour from such a fine creature, he secretly loved it. He loved the attention. He loved music. In fact he had pressed play on the tape of his favourite band, *The Necessities*, so many times that the tape had warped so badly that he had had to use a twig to untangle it. It still played, yet the singer's voice wavered and warbled and trembled as the tape played. He didn't mind though. He also loved the feeling of lust and longing and awe and wonder and fear that sometimes were all mixed up together, that he saw in the eyes of the humans who watched. This was a long time ago. No idea how he got hold of a cassette machine. But it doesn't matter.

Now, one day whilst the bear was dancing his furry ass off at the local market, the stream was comforting the little girl. The girl was feeling blue. Even her pigtails looked sad, hanging limp down her back. She was sad because she missed her family. It was never clear as to whether she was truly an orphan, as the bear who had rescued her when she was young had told her, or whether she was an orphan because the bear had accidentally, or more likely purposely, eaten her whole family. Her mother. Her father. And her two sisters.

With the songs she normally sang not making a dent on the little girl's mood, the stream told her that if she was missing her sisters, whom the girl loved playing with, then why not imagine that they were there with her now? The stream told the little girl that all she needed to do was to picture them perfectly in her mind. Every detail. She also said that she could make them into whatever she wanted them to be. She was the mistress of her imagination after all.

The little girl was immediately moved from her morose thoughts, into the excitement that possibility creates. And, because she was only a little girl after all, she decided that her sisters, and by that very fact, herself, were actually from an aristocratic family from the North of the country. Russia if you were wondering. And that they had special powers. As did she. And that they would live forever and never ever die again because it hurt too much in her tummy and because she was lonely without them.

And so, it came to be that the very next day, at roughly the same time, though there were no clocks back in those days, whilst the bear was wiggling his hips suggestively at the local market, the two sisters appeared out of nowhere besides the stream where the little girl spent her days alone. As one can imagine, the sisters did not first appear in their solid form. This was, after all, the workings of a lonely girl's mind. No. At first they appeared as apparitions, hazy, transparent, ethereal figures, just an essence of their full selves. With the assistance of the stream, the little girl focused harder, screwing up her hazel eyes and concentrating intensely, willing these shadowy ghosts into being. Into being human.

It worked. And as they gained substance, and realised where they were, they were startled at first, and a bit afraid of the bear, who by now had returned and was taking a well earned nap, until the little girl told them how kind he was. It wasn't long before the three of them laughed and played and it was all great until the little girl drowned one day in the stream, which felt a little bitchy, let's be honest, and the two sisters decided that they were far too real now for fairytale and forest living anymore and so set off to the nearest city and into the big wide world.

How the Harpist fell in love with music and met her Maestro, is a tale for another day. And how the

Immortal Woman ended up an addict in the nasty business of stealing other people's life force, is also a story for another other day.

Suffice to say that the two sisters were only alive because once upon a time a little girl imagined them that way.

So, if you take anything from this, let it be a warning. Be careful what you imagine into being.

Oh, and if you were wondering. The answer is yes. They are far from being the only magical creatures that are living in the world. Remember that the next time you're walking down your city streets. Maybe if we stopped looking down at the ground or at our phones or being so far in the future or the past in our minds that we actually took notice, we would see a lot more than what we believe to be true.

Anyways, where were we? Aaah yes.

The Harpist knew people. Who knew people. Who knew other people. Who knew. And so, having thought about it long and hard, she sat her sister down one day and placed a piece of paper on the table exactly equidistant from them both. It was the exact location for where the Deer Woman was. In coordinates. As soon as the Immortal Woman realised what it was, she snatched the paper and sprang up from her chair causing it to fly backwards. She placed a kiss on the top of her sister's head, began cackling and muttering to herself, donned her coat and hat, and slammed the door shut behind her - leaving the Harpist in the whirl of the aftermath and a disquieting feeling that that might not have been the best idea she'd ever had.

By the time that the Immortal Woman found her way to the woods of Alderley Edge, it was late, very late. The air was holding its breath. It didn't take her long to find where the Deer Woman lived, as the pull towards her that she had originally felt had heightened intensely over the months that she had been gone. Yet, standing near a cluster of trees, it didn't look like anyone lived there. It was of course dark, and the Immortal Woman had to find her way by reading the silhouettes cast by the light of the silvery moon. At first glance it appeared that there was nothing but trees in this forest. But then, she thought that she could see the Deer Woman sleeping. Her eyes closed. Perched up against a tree, sat on a cushion of moss, with a blanket of sewn leaves and grasses, her antlers, now huge, wrapped lazily around the trunk as if they were lovers idling an embrace as they slept. Though, as the Immortal Woman peered closer, she realised that it was an illusion, and her heart dropped for a brief moment. However, looking closer still, there seemed to be a shard of light emanating from between the chimerical antlers. As she leaned in further, a little cautious with each step, she could swear she heard the sounds of people talking. Of laughter. Of the chink of glass upon glass. Of ceramic against ceramic. Of china against china. And of music.

How odd! she thought. And came in closer towards the tree. She pressed her ear against its trunk and was surprised to find that the sounds sharpened, and the tree vibrated against her ear. Without thinking about it, she reached over to - what appeared to be - the antlers and running her hands across them, admiring their velvet coat, and feeling a thrill through her fingertips, she accidentally pressed the tips of the antlers together. The trunk slid apart, as if quite naturally, and an elevator appeared before her. Oddly, it seemed that it was expecting her. She got in and seeing that there were no buttons, simply waited. The doors closed and the elevator began to move.

But not up nor down.

The elevator appeared to move sideways. Or rather, it seemed to be going round and round, as if drawing circles with itself around the inside of the tree trunk.

Obviously, this was all ludicrous. However, the Immortal Woman began to feel as if they were descending as her ears began to pop with the change of air pressure, she realised that they were indeed spiralling around and down, down and around. Until they stopped. And the doors opened. The Immortal Woman stood for a moment, eyes blinking wildly and widely, as she was oh so unprepared for what she was seeing.

The elevator doors had opened to reveal a bar. Not just any old bar mind you. But a Speakeasy bar. With live beetles as door handles, that when called upon, busied themselves with bringing ingredients out of little drawers and jars. Butterflies buzzing around dancing for pleasure and entertainment. Tarantula spiders as bouncers. And crickets, dressed to the nines, crooning jazz riffs, on a stage to the side.

And the Deer Woman in all of her splendour, behind the bar, wiping a cup, a ceramic china one of course, with a tea towel.

You look tired. Tea?

If one could imagine the sensation of being inside the whirling dervish force of a tornado right now, with the wind cutting your skin with the feeling of a trillion tiny silver blades, no bigger than a whisker from your chin. And if one could imagine the sound was like being in the very nucleus particle of that initial big bang, you know, the one where the whole goddamn world was created. Then, perhaps, you'd have the slightest sense of what the Immortal Woman was experiencing within her being. And this time, it was not for the Deer Woman herself, but for who she now so obviously was, without a shadow of a doubt, despite appearances that might cause that doubt. A deer. Well, a deer and a woman to be completely clear. A deer woman.

All of the Immortal Woman's life force receptors had switched on as brightly as they possibly could.

Deer.

Through all of her living over all of the centuries, no matter how extraordinary it had been, it had also given her time, plenty of it, to understand more about immortality. Because you would, wouldn't you? Considering you and it were bonded for the longest time. Forever. Onwards to infinity you both go. And one of the things that she had learned, and known of, for all these moments, is that the key to being released from immortality, is held by the deer.

But there's a catch. Of course there's a catch.

The deer has to willingly give you its life force.

It has to intentionally entrust and gift you with its life. And that's a pretty big ask and task, of animal or human, never mind a stranger. Not only that, but if you take the life force of a deer, without the above stipulations, then you risk sickness. A sickness so overpowering and frightful, that even the thought of having that experience again, is enough to reassure any deer out there that they were safe.

The Immortal Woman had caught that rarest of possibilities, a gem of the impossible, that day at the museum, but had never allowed herself to believe it could be true. She couldn't allow herself to, because the idea that this was not the case would have opened her old, twisted, but bright and healthy heart right up, and she had had to close it shut and suture it with one of her sister's old heartstrings, as the pain of never being able to physically embrace another, never mind kiss all down their body, or hold their hand as you sat silently together, was too much for her to bear. Sure, she had immortality. But at a price. Immortality has never been the best hugger.

The deer held the powers of regeneration and a resurgence of heart and life energy. And their medicine was stored in their antlers. As one can imagine, the very freakish nature of the Deer Woman's antlers, which by now were akin to a tree themselves, was practically a powerhouse of life force, buzzing that electric hum that was making the Immortal Woman vibrate violently in ecstasy.

Violent ecstasy. The key to mortality. To death. And oh boy, she was ready for that time. She was tired. Done. Every part of her being filled with the memories that she took, and the feelings raced around her body on an endless track of everything a human could possibly feel. It was a lot. She was done.

I am. Tired. And she smiled at the Deer Woman, who had offered her a tea, lavender, for her nerves. As the truth of that washed over her, just like that, all of her madness melted away, leaving a puddle on the floor under where she sat on the stool made out of branches. Her eyes were soft, and wet too. She looked young then, only a child. A child who was brought back to life, to the world, without her permission.

I know what you want. The Deer Woman sat across from her. She seemed older, different in her face. She looked ancient in fact. And peaceful. Very peaceful. As if she were so rooted to the earth that she was still. So still. A fact that the Immortal Woman could feel. It was mesmerising.

And I also knew that you would come. One day.

You just disappeared, poof! You left no tracks. No scents or movement, it's as if you disappeared off the face of the earth. You didn't exist.

But you knew that I hadn't though, didn't you? You're still here. You opened your heart to me and there was a crack. I felt it too. And that would never do. You let hope seep through like sap. And now you're here.

Where did you go?

Everywhere. And nowhere.

The Deer Woman rested her arms on the bar. Her downy arms, which were red, spotted with white patches. As were her hands, though her fingers were still of human form.

I learned some things from the deer once, at the beginning, when I first left and didn't know where to go. I felt so unsettled. They taught me about invisibility. How to look like you're not there. They, humans, can't see you. They just don't have the capacity.

The Deer Woman reached out and took the Immortal Woman's left hand in hers.

No! What are you doing? She tried to yank it back wondering if it was too late and the sickness was in her already.

But the Deer Woman held tight.

Shhhh. It's ok. It's ok. Look. She looked down at their hands. The Immortal Woman did too. *You can't take anything from me. It's all in here.* And she tapped her antlers gently.

I have something for you. I was expecting you.

The Deer Woman reached up to the highest shelf behind her at the bar. In the corner an iridescent beetle, of pinks, and blues and purples, was busy opening up a drawer for her hand to slip into. When she pulled it out, she held a small pouch, which had something in it.

More tea?

The Deer Woman brought the teapot on to the bar, careful to put down a doily spun with the dreams of spiders, before she placed it down. She reached up with both hands and with a knowing only she could have, chose two of the finest, boniest, china cups that the Immortal Woman had ever seen.

She poured two cups of tea and then opened the pouch. Inside there was a powder, coarse, and ashen grey. She poured all of it into the Immortal Woman's cup and gave it a stir with a tiny golden spoon. She pushed the cup, on its matching saucer, over to her.

Drink.

The Immortal Woman lifted the cup to her lips and held it there. She looked over at the Deer Woman, tears in her eyes once more. *Thank you. I'm sorry.* She said these last two words as if as a prayer. For a lifetime of robbery.

The powder from the Deer Woman's fallen antlers of previous seasons started to take effect immediately. The Immortal Woman began to see the memories. All of them. She could feel every emotion in every one of them. Countless lives flashing before her eyes, but not hers. Not yet anyways. A kaleidoscope of memories. She weeps for each of them, her heart swelling so big that it cannot contain itself anymore, and just before she thinks that this is it, she sees another memory. It's of a little girl, and two others. And a big house. And a pony. And parties with dressing up boxes. And laughter. And it's hers.

She can feel it. And just like that, her heart bursts her into a thousand and one pieces, which the small rodents, busy to keep the floor clean, eat away at until there is only bone left. And her bones dry out as fast as it takes to take a deep breath in, until all that is left is dust.

The Deer Woman finishes her own tea at this point. She picks up the Immortal Woman's cup and kisses it.

8.

Curiouser and curiouser.

When her sister failed to return from her mission to find the Deer Woman, the Harpist grew more and more concerned as to what might have happened to her. Sure, she had often disappeared for days, weeks, months, even years, before. Suddenly reappearing without warning just as brusquely as she had disappeared. Though the Harpist kept telling her how frustrating that was and how all she wanted was to be told that she was going away, or an odd postcard or two to land in her letterbox, this pattern of behaviour never changed. It had occurred to the Harpist that perhaps her sister never actually intended to disappear. Maybe she was only ever going out to the shops to buy bread or milk or lemons or apples or sherry. And then something happened on the way to the marketplace. Which sounded like a bad joke. Yet this time, obviously, she knew where her sister had gone, and the fact that she had neither seen, nor heard from her since, filled her with dread.

This dread crept up her sleeves, and her collar, and as it began to feel its way, clammy, uneasy, up her leg, the Harpist started to feel anxious.

And when she felt anxious, which to be honest, was rather rare, the Harpist would first turn to her cards. Those wisdom cards, as the Maestro had appointed them, shuffling the pack before spreading them out in a dramatic flourish on the table before her. The Harpist would indulge the Maestro with this sensational activity, which he implemented daily, though for her it was all such nonsense. A silly little game to occupy those silly little human foibles for all things magic and mysterious. If only they knew. For though she never had to partake of such soul snatching activities as her sister to remain alive, it was rather remarkable that at the age of thirty, the Harpist simply stopped ageing. Of course, her sister would curse her over the years, fondly and playfully at first, and then as the decades passed, her curses would land with a resentful blow, for not only was the Harpist blessed to remain at an age where her beauty was at its peak - whilst the Immortal Woman had to continuously strive to look as young and as attractive as her sister - she was also devouringly promiscuous, courting everything under the sun. Her forays into carnal matters didn't affect the chosen human in the same manner as the Immortal Woman's solicitations did, and this only added to the Immortal Woman's venom towards her sister. Unkind words. Unruly behaviour. And at times, though the Harpist would scold her with such ferocity that this behaviour paused for a brief spell, the Immortal Woman would consciously seek out her sister's lover du jour and make sure that she 'accidentally' stole a large portion of their life force.

Not the kind of conduct deemed appropriate for such an immortal being. Though, the Harpist was familiar with the scorning and scouring revenge afoot in those tales of the Greek and Roman gods, so she suspected that her sister was just following in their mischievous footsteps.

Still, despite their petty, and at times grandiose disagreements, she loved her sister greatly, and so, as was her way, the Harpist sought to find out more.

She spread the tarot deck out, which she had admittedly sought solace in after the Maestro's death, and chose three cards. Frowning, her foot tapped rapidly against the wooden tiles beneath as she surveyed the cards.

Death. The Tower. 3 of Swords.

The Harpist shook her head, swallowing hard so as not to allow the mix of bile and tears that threatened to overwhelm her. Those first two cards did not bode well. For though they could represent the end of one chapter and the remaking and resurrection of a life, she knew instinctively that this time they meant what they said on the tin – literal death and the destruction of all that sustained the life it took.

It was the third card that gave her a glimmer and a shimmer of hope though. The three swords that pierced through the heart in the image, reminded her of the arrows that her sister would mournfully, yet stubbornly, collect, from those she romanced. Over time, the Immortal Woman had become a devoted student of - as ironic though that that might be - Cupid. Not just for the hopeful longing and yearning for love, but for the arrows that Cupid would send soaring to penetrate the heart of the one suddenly struck by this godly intervention.

For the weird thing was, the Immortal Woman could actually see these arrows – to her they weren't simply a manner of speech, but real, wooden, finely crafted implements. Each arrow, carefully curated, driven precisely and cleanly, into human flesh.

She discovered that it didn't impact the one Cupid had chosen, if she was to remove the arrow when in her human lover's intimate company. Over time she had learned how to do so without causing distress to the person they had struck. She usually assumed this activity when the other was asleep. Though of course, she would be putting the one she craved in deathly danger by staying overnight to embrace the body she had made love with and given not such a little death to, and so, as the human lay dreaming, the Immortal Woman would slowly free the arrow, and leave with this token of love. Back home, she would deposit the arrow in a vase on a desk in her bedroom, as if these arrows were flowers cut from a fucked up Hallmark darkened garden. These Cupid's arrows - real, not symbolic - had each once been lodged inside a human heart that had caught feelings for the Immortal Woman. Upon awakening, with memories and body still caught in the scent and touch of the last night's lover, they would shake off the feeling of amorous appetite that had nearly consumed them, simply believing that love had only momentarily come to visit, and as such, had now moved through and on. To the next they supposed, sighing whilst collapsing back on to their bed, their hand gently rubbing at the ache at their heart.

At times, often after her latest romance went awry because she took all of their life force when kissing – again – the Immortal Woman would lie in her bed at night, the arrow from that last love held tight, breathing in the scent of rotting flesh that she never cleaned off from the tip where it had speared their heart. As much as her sister had pleaded with her to at least wash said arrows before bringing them into their home, the Immortal Woman refused.

For love never lasted, and the lovers came and went. Only the arrows remained. Solid. Strong. Each one carrying a whole story of its own.

Such as the gardener for the Royal Courts. Their eyes had met whilst she was her sister's plus one for a day party honouring the Harpist. Later the gardener and the Immortal Woman had swapped saliva, fingers and hands roaming and searching, amidst the rose bushes at the back of the east garden. For each week of their affair, the gardener had gifted her with a different rose, which the Immortal Woman, never terribly au fait with how to handle living things, would instantly press the flower until any remnant of life had been squashed. She still kept these petals in a wooden box on her dresser, and still chose upon occasion to feel the soft satin petals between her fingers as she had done so with the gardener herself.

Or the sailor she had met whilst living out her '*Sinbad on the high seas*' fantasy. He was brutish and charming, all black beard and a portly belly. His eyes bore into hers and she would become flushed and modest and he would have his way with her on land and upon the seas. His particular thrill was for fucking on the top deck amidst a storm. As was his way, he preferred being on top, and unfortunately for him, the last time they had been at it whilst the wind blew and the sea showered them with its own salts, the mast broke and the boom knocked him swiftly and without time to say adios, into the cold, deep sea. He never even bobbed to the surface, despite her waiting for him to do so until the dawn rose. His arrow smelled like shanties and scotch and its aroma still made her panties moist.

Then there was the one that got away. A tailor from Toronto. They had spent a summer, autumn and half a winter touring the Canadian cities, wearing the finest suits and stockings, and making out in their cabins all afternoon. This one, sadly, ended up as a desiccated heart in their fridge for the Harpist to find.

The Immortal Woman had literally loved them to death.

As the Harpist mused on her sister's array of disastrous romances, she couldn't help but consider that maybe the card was telling her something else, other than disappointment and heartbreak, which she was feeling right at that moment.

A few months back, she had invited two of her musical fans - they had their uses and would do anything for her - to the place where she'd sent her sister, Alderley Edge, asking them to see if they could find the 'woman who lived in the woods', a local folktale that she was curious to know of its veracity. Yet, they had returned shaking their heads that they had found nothing of the sort out there.

Luckily, the Harpist had skills. Skills gained from the fortuitously extravagant and remarkable life, or maybe that should read lives, that she had lived. She had worked with the intelligence service a few decades ago – that rumour happened to be true – and so she knew how to gather and garner information.

So, she started her search in the place most known to her sister: her bedroom, which was a mess of papers, sheaves scattered in no apparent pattern, all about her room. Pages of scrawl that the Immortal Woman thought would assist in helping to empty her mind of oh so many of their memories – the ones she fed from - lest they were to become so heavy that she would fall to the ground encumbered and be unable to stand ever again.

Most of the pages were unreadable. Nonsensical scribbles that made no sense.

The Harpist gave up attempting to decipher them and instead began to open and rifle through the drawers by her bed. It was in the bottom drawer that she found her sister's diary. Well, the thick notebook, marked SECRET on it with large, purple sharpie lettering. *Subtle,* thought the Harpist dryly as she sat on the bed and opened it.

The Immortal Woman had been busy. Every page was filled with notes, references, information. Some pages had articles snipped and clipped from newspapers stapled or glued on to them, yellowing and frayed, dissolving back into the ether with each movement of the notebook in the Harpist's hands. The book was a memoriam to immortality, and the quest, and request, to find a way to leave.

The Harpist paused in her frenzied page turning and set the book to her lap. Tears welled up in her eyes, and she began to sob. Though she knew that her sister suffered tremendously over her fate, she hadn't been privy to the fact that she was damn well doing something about it. The Harpist felt a brief sting at her heart as she realised that there were things that the Immortal Woman had deliberately kept as a secret from her. She shrugged this off immediately. It was ok to have secrets, wasn't it?

in Manchester. Watching this show had been a favoured activity of both sisters once upon a time, and this fact created an ache at the Harpist's heart. She wasn't fully watching it though, as her mind was wandering from one point to another, desperately attempting to fill in the gaps. Unsuccessfully. But it was when the words .... *most likely a glass vial manufactured by the Romanian House of Mirrors...* sounded out from the television, that she sat up straight, turned up the volume, and listened more attentively.

Andy McConnell was holding a glass vial in his hands, turning it slowly, allowing the camera to pan over the gilded detailing across the base of the vial. He was explaining how this was an unusual find, and with an excited voice he commented on the scene of a dancing bear and three little girls holding hands that made up the base in such refined and miniature expertise. The Harpist was only half hearing his words, spoken in that plummy posh British accent, as her hands began to shake, and the colour drained from her face. The vial was not empty, the host was saying, and he tilted it to show the cameras the small amount of water still contained in it. He asked the gentleman who had brought it in if he'd taken a sip and they all laughed. When asked as to where he had obtained such a rare and perfect item, the gentleman explained that it was his daughter who had found it whilst they were out walking in the woods near to their home.

The Harpist remained frozen in her seat. A wave of realisation hit her then, for her sister always wore that vial around her neck. She didn't take it off, not even to wash. The fact that it was found abandoned in the woods, the place where she had foolishly sent the Immortal Woman, made her gasp and cry out in pain.

Guilt and rage permeated her mind, so that her vision became blurred, overcome with such emotion. The guilt subsided to a low thrumming pulse, whilst the rage heightened, sharpened, threatening to burn her up into a crisp.

Now, she thought, a sudden shard of clarity hitting her mind, this is personal.

9.

The Harpist's revenge

It was nine months later, from the day the Immortal Woman had turned to dust, that the Harpist set out to find her sister. This time she didn't need to contact someone, who knew someone, to know where the Deer Woman lived, for the Harpist had managed to track her down herself, using sleuth, stealth, and salubrious salutations. Though the Deer Woman was no longer living in the woods, she hadn't travelled far. For despite having successfully given up the Speakeasy bar in a tree that she'd built - to an owl who didn't mind one jot that the work was after hours - she had moved only a few miles down the road, and into the gardens of an eccentric billionaire scientist who lived in Sale.

The Scientist had twenty acres of land, including the woods that the Deer Woman now inhabited, and had pretty much left nature to do its own thing, barely visiting said woods as his preoccupation, read obsession, with the microscopic world that he loved, meant that he was much more contented to be leant over a microscope studying slides of all matter of matter. For instance, right now he was studying the nature of human tears. He would make himself cry with varying emotions and collect the teardrops and spend hours, days, weeks, gazing dreamily at them magnified beyond human comprehension. He loved the crystalline snowflakes that each formed as the tear dried leaving its residue of salt. He suspected how this was akin to those mumbo-jumbo tea leaf readings his younger sister was into on YouTube, and which he rolled his eyes at, as if his way was better. He found stark differences to the patterns of these salt snowflakes in the tears of joy to those of sadness. Tears of anger and frustration to those of care and compassion. It was the latter of these that he was most concerned with, for the Scientist, ambitious in his ideals, was convinced that the right kind of human tears could replenish the oceans that, in a political era of climate despair, were found to be evaporating.

It was purely by chance on one of her twice-yearly trips to Cheshire to visit the Scientist, that the Harpist got wind, metaphorically and literally, that the Deer Woman must be nearby. She had befriended the Scientist many years ago at a charitable polo match when they had both discovered a mutual fascination with tears and, with more than enough herself, had agreed to supply him with those that she had no use for, to aid in his research.

You could say it was a coincidence.

Yet in reality, it was a drawing.

One that a crow had deposited on the kitchen table where the Scientist and the Harpist were sitting having lunch. The crow had flown through the open French windows in the salon and had swooped and soared across the hallway until dropping the drawing on the table, before swooping and soaring away again. Though this startled the Harpist, the Scientist took it in his stride, which makes one assume he was accustomed to such behaviour.

The drawing was of a bear. Eating honey and fish. An odd and unsavoury combination sure, yet the bear had a blissful look on his face. Now this might have had nothing to do with anything apart from one detail – a small, red cassette player was positioned by his feet, and the artist had drawn little dashes emanating from it, as if it was playing its music.

The Harpist snatched the paper from the table and brought it close to her nose and sniffed it. It was then that she was certain, as certain as any strange character in a strange story can be, that the Deer Woman was there, hiding in the Scientist's estate. How did she know this with such certainty? She could smell the scent of her sister – old flesh, violet and leather – and the Harpist would know that scent anywhere.

Inquiring as to whether the Scientist had noticed any unusual activity on his grounds, he vigorously shook his head, for if truth be told, he had no time, nor inclination, nor need, to wander the grounds of his mansion, his laboratory being his sole solace. Which was a shame. His mansion was left to him by an uncle who had won a Nobel Prize for something to do with gravity and noble noses, or so it was said, and he had never even heard of this uncle, a Professor Stirling, before receiving news of his death. As the Scientist was the only male in the family - note, there were plenty of women, mind - all of this uncle's great fortune, including said home, went to him. To be honest, it overwhelmed him often and he'd get panic attacks and have to put himself to bed for a week. In many ways, being born a sensitive soul with such a nervous disposition, was the perfect constitution for one who spends his days marvelling at the profound beauty of other worlds. He found other humans strange and perplexing and so he lived alone and had no problem with being the hermit that lives on that big estate in Cheshire.

For the Deer Woman, it meant that she hadn't needed to put effort into being invisible in the way that the deer had taught her, and which was rather exhausting to implement on a daily basis, and instead she could be free. There were no visitors, tourists, teenage witch wannabees or serious weekend middle-aged walkers to contend with. Just her. The animals. And the trees.

Truth be told, she'd felt a little undone since the Immortal Woman's visit. A change of scenery was sure to help clear her mind and give her the ideal tonic to move on. But it hadn't helped to be fair. And on that particular day, she heard the Harpist coming from five and twenty miles away.

And she could smell her too. For the closer the Harpist got; fear began to creep up the Deer Woman's antlers. There was another scent too. One that made her pulse begin to race, and her hind legs - well, just her legs really - begin to tense ready to take flight. And the smell got stronger, until the ability to flee had passed and now she was simply frozen to the spot. As startled as a deer could possibly ever be.

The Deer Woman had some of the Immortal Woman's ashes around her neck, ironically in the same small pouch which had previously housed the grounds of the last season's antlers, which she had been saving for their final use. The few moments where she'd held the hand of the Immortal Woman had not been without its repercussions, as the addictive part of the Immortal Woman's nature had snaked its way into the life force of the Deer Woman. What that meant was that she had taken to snorting the Immortal Woman's ashes, like a heart-broken lover inhaling the bones of the one they had lost.

There was another consequence to snorting the Immortal Woman's ashes – she'd ingested her memories too. All of them. Darting deliriously about in her brain. The more she increasingly inhaled the fine grey powder, the stronger she communed with these images in her mind. This was, as you might well imagine, terribly confusing for the Deer Woman.

And so, she spent a lot of her time tripping out in the woods on these ashes, and drawing pictures of her visions, which incidentally, bar the one gifted by the crow, many years later, the scientist would find. Mystified as to how they had ended up on his land and who was the mysterious artist, he had them published in a book that lived on the coffee tables of people worldwide. She seemed to have struck a chord with the dreamers and the William Blake lovers, and over time, this anonymous artist would sit beside Leonora Carrington and Hilma af Klint as one of the finest Surrealists that had ever lived. But that's too far into the future for us now, so let's return back to the woods, and to the Deer Woman, who by now was paralysed to the spot.

The Harpist knew that she had to be clever if she had any chance of getting close to the Deer Woman. She knew how fast she could run, leap, and jump and how strong she was. Perusing the list of substances deemed poisonous to a deer, she had lavished herself with everything Elderberry, one of the most toxic of them all. Elderberry oil from The Body Shop, and Elderberry body lotion from Boots, and strings and garlands of Elderberries in various states of trauma from the hot footing it to get there the Harpist had just done. They'd been jostled and crushed and squeezed and many of them had become ghosts of their former selves, their skins hanging, their sweet purple syrup blood staining the white Whistles shirtdress that the Harpist was wearing so that she looked, quite honestly, ridiculous. But it worked.

The Deer Woman was stunned.

And that's when she heard it.

Before she felt it.

There was a loud thudding sound that rocked her whole body, and then the echo of that thud reverberating through the trees.

And then the pain hit.

Looking towards her left shoulder, the Deer Woman noticed an arrow sticking out of her. That's strange, she thought before the reality of the situation hit her with its sharp and precise pain. She cried out. A raw roar that released a flock of bats who had made their home for the evening in the trees around her as the light was of the dusk, and all the animals tended to rest at this point and enjoy the shifting into the night.

And then the same happened again. To her right shoulder this time. Pinning her to the trunk of the oak tree she was resting against, rivulets of blood seeping, like tears, down her dress. The Deer Woman cried out even more furiously this time. In excruciating agony.

The Harpist came into view before her watering eyes. A blur to begin with, then the form of this woman whom she realised was the Harpist from that concert she'd attended with the Immortal Woman. What was she doing here? It didn't make any sense. Yet at the same time, there was something deeply familiar about her, something more, well, intimate.

They're cupid's arrows. The Harpist spoke. *She kept each and every one that had struck the heart of every lover she had tried to get close to but had accidentally killed. Drained of their life force, each and every time, over all those years. So many arrows, all moaning under the weight of cupid's fetish. Of her inability to have the one thing that she thought might make the rest of her indeterminable life, remotely happy. Hah to that hey?! Where is she? What did you do to her?*

The Deer Woman reached up her hand to the pouch without her realising it, holding the contents tight in her hand.

She smiled. *I set her free. Isn't that what she always wanted? It was either I set her free, or she would kill me and slowly destroy herself in the process. This seemed fairer.*

The Deer Woman coughed then cried out once again into the thick, silent, cool night air.

The Harpist drew another arrow. It was covered in dark thick pieces of flesh. Flesh that had dried out over the years and become rotted into the wooden steel of the arrow. It had hardened as all things cast out do and had settled in as its new identity alongside the arrow itself.

I learnt this from my Maestro. The Harpist was examining the cupid's arrow she'd pulled from its quiver. Archery. *The steadiness of both hands and attention. He had this picture in his room. There was nothing else…not really. But this…this always caught my gaze for a brief moment or two.*

For a moment all was still, bar an owl hooting nearby. The Harpist was calm, composed, clear. No rush. No rush. She stepped nearer to the Deer Woman now, towering over her.

It mesmerised me, she continued, before pulling out a card from her pocket. The Harpist glanced at the card before flinging it on to the Deer Woman, where it landed on her skirt, image facing upwards.

He explained to me that it was an image from tarocchi, or tarot as it's more commonly known. An image that upon first glance caused me to breathe in deeply, with its big fat heart pierced with three arrows. It looked like it would hurt, that many cuts, don't you think? But then they do say that the truth hurts, right?

The Deer Woman winced as she looked up at the Harpist, unable to move and blinded by pain.

That image had always intrigued and disgusted me equally, but I had understood its truer meaning over the years. I understood that a heart that had never been pierced, had never loved. Its song always told the truth. And it was beautiful. It is beautiful.

At these last words she looked down at the Deer Woman, her face cold and as steel as her arrows.

I think you owe her something. In exchange for her life. Don't you agree? I mean, she was your elder...

What?

And seeing as you seem to have snorted most of her up your nose over the last few months, you're mostly her now anyways, aren't you?!

The Harpist had taken a guess as she said that, but something about the frenzied movement of the Deer Woman, whom she'd been watching closely for some time before drawing that first arrow, reminded her of her sister's own erratic behaviour. As it turns out, by the look on the Deer Woman's face, she was right.

So. You're coming with me. You're my sister too now!

The Deer Woman looked startled, again, and a single tear fell from her left eye.

It's you. You...you're... my... Sister?!

The Harpist nodded, more softly this time, and spoke in kinder words.

Yes. I didn't realise it at first. Why did you have such an impact upon her? I'd never seen anything like it before. And then after she disappeared, I did some research. Some...how do I put this...some shit that you would never understand...being you're a...was...a human that is.

I'm not? Is that what you're saying? The Deer Woman winced as she spoke. Her brow was dappled in beads of sweat; her temperature was rising. The pain was worse now.

Yes. You are. Human that is. You're her. Back. Back for another go around the sun as we say. It took a long time, but it's you. Born again. Natural. It was in your tears. The same pattern as mine. My friend, and the man whose home you're illegally squatting in, told me.

At this point the Harpist told her everything that she had uncovered over the last few months. How it had all begun that evening when seeing a glass vial, her glass vial, on that show. It had never occurred to the Harpist to give her careful attention to that part of the vial – the pattern on the base, which had been hand rendered in such exquisite detail.

As Mister McConnell had pointed out on the show, *the Romanian House of Mirrors* had mysteriously closed in 1877, and so no more of their wares were ever made. Yet, every year since, an anonymous package would arrive for her from the glass makers. The Harpist would open up the gift, extravagantly and carefully wrapped, to find another glass vial. She had had some of these looked over by glass experts over the years and everyone had attested to the fact that they were originals. Having seen the vial on the antiques roadshow - which she had paid the gentleman who had it a tidy gargantuan sum for its recovery - she had gathered all of the gifted vials from the last one hundred and twenty-three years, stored in boxes, cupboards and on display in her living room - one hundred and twenty-three vials - and had studied each and every one. It was around the time of the hundred and seventh vial that she knew. With every single bone in her body and every single hair on her head, that this was her story. Her story, her sister, the Immortal Woman's story, and their other sister, the Deer Woman's story. Engraved as a puzzle, hiding in plain sight, for all the world to see.

The Deer Woman looked up at her older sister. She knew these words were true even though she had no memory of them herself. Well, not prior to acquiring her newly formed snorting habit that is. Yet oddly enough, as the Harpist was speaking, vivid details formed in the Deer Woman's mind, so real, so true. As she closed her eyes, she recalled the sound of the stream singing a song strange to her ears. The smell of the bear's skin, woody, earthy, faintly animal, as she lay curled in in its embrace. She could feel it. Remember it. Remember a wish, so painfully and strikingly pierced itself with the arrow of deep sadness, for companionship, friendship and family. For the love of her sisters. She opened her eyes and gazed softly at the Harpist, who had drawn one more arrow back in its bow. She held it there as her words landed in the Deer Woman's heart.

A sister's love that you only know if you know. And now, she wanted to make a wrong into a right. To make it all equal. It was only fair.

But it wasn't. The Deer Woman started to cry this time. And she sobbed, big ugly sobs, like a child. A young girl, alone in the woods with just a bear and a stream for company.

Her breath felt laboured, and she felt sick and dizzy, as if she was drowning, in a stream. These were her last thoughts as the sound of the thud and the echo happened one more time.

The third arrow had struck exactly the centre of her chest.

10.

The End?

The Harpist stood and bowed and had roses strewn all around her. The applause was like the sound of a roar. She tried not to think about it. Since she had killed the Deer Woman, she had kept her heart in a jar and brought it out on stage to hypnotise the audience at every show so that their tears just flowed and flowed like nobody's business. Her reputation had launched itself off into outer space. Into the timeless itself.

She missed her sister dreadfully. Yet, she had to keep going. For the earth needed the beauty that leaked out of the hearts of her audience. It was what kept enchantment and the possibility of being bewitched alive. Otherwise, wonder and magic would dry up and there would be no water, and nothing could live on parched earth, and that would mean that there'd be no stream that meandered around where a little girl once lived with the bear.

And that would mean there would be no reason for this tale to be happening. Or any of those other tales, that seem off kilter to you or I but are happening right now on aisle three in Aldi down the road.

And so, there would be no need for imagination. What a horror that would be.

Now, you might be left wondering why they didn't have more exciting lives. The thing is, they did, fabulous lives, eventful and adventurous and rich and sumptuous, until the Harpist fell in love with music, and with playing the harp. Like, seriously in love. That she chose instead of frolicking forever across the world, to devote and dedicate all of her time to learning her craft.

And because she was the sole guardian of her sister, the Immortal Woman, the latter sort of just followed her around. Kept close by. The Immortal Woman had never much ambition for anything in particular after many centuries took them for a ride. So, she just got a job for something to do. It was a bonus that she actually did love working at the museum. And let's face it, she had her appetites and ways of getting off on life. She enjoyed herself. Mainly.

As for the Deer Woman, ironically, she ended up at the museum that had started her destiny's clock ticking in the first place. As she was both horrifying and enchanting, she had her own special room. A dark square space with her as the centrepiece, a light above her, casting its brilliance over her and delicately gracing the golden shining plaque with the newly engraved words: "Be careful what you use your Imagination for!"

Her head, neck and shoulders had been mounted on a thick block of walnut wood. A deep red velvet, both in feel and colour, behind her. The glass case was ever so long and ever so high, capturing the magnificence of her antlers. Her face, with its glassy eyes, peering at you. Could she somehow see you? This weird half woman, half deer thing. What in God's name is it?! Many would leave the room unsettled. Some though saw her beauty, and that would stay with them forever.

She had been an anonymous gift left on the doorstep one night and which now drew crowds the likes of which the museum has never seen before.

And it wasn't long before the weather got into its weird shit again, and the world tilted a little this way and a little that way.

The Harpist didn't notice. For she was much more concerned with the odd fact that now, for the very first time in the whole of her long life, she was beginning to age. Just like every other human being.

And back on Oxford Road, on the second floor of a mahogany crafted room, in the grandest, some might say, museum of them all, a young man was wiping his bloodied finger which had caught on a rusted nail and shaking his head at the disbelief that the tiger on display, forever captured all open-mouthed and sabre-toothed, had apparently winked at him.

It would only be a few days later that he would start to feel a strange aching in his jaw.

As they say, and good heavens they say a lot, nature is indeed a most curious fellow.

The End.

About the Author

Heidi Hinda Chadwick is a writer drawn to the weird, the feral, and the quietly unsettling. She loves to explore the psychological intricacies of human experience, often drawing on folklore, psychology, body horror, femgore, twisting traditional fairytales and exploring contemporary anxieties.

Her influences include Mona Awad, Bora Chung, Sayaka Murata, Ottessa Moshfegh, Eliza Clark, and feminist horror writers such as Mariana Enriquez, all of whom place ordinary people in unnervingly altered worlds. Heidi Hinda is particularly interested in what lies beneath the polished surface of human life: desire, obsession, power, and the beauty of the unbeautiful.

Heidi publishes essays, and articles on life, love, eros, art, horror, creativity, and the uncomfortable edges of being human, and is currently enjoying writing strange macabre tales seeped in reality. She describes herself first and foremost as a storyteller, driven by curiosity about the world and what it means to be human.

Heidi writes short stories and novellas, works as a creative wellbeing consultant and trauma-informed artist & educator, is an embodied performer and speaker, a writing mentor for *Elephant Journal*, and is a member of Manchester Women's Writers and the European Jaguar Writers Groups. She believes creativity is a form of revolution and is passionate about championing independent, emerging voices and creative freedom.

She's been published in *Agave*, *SheHub*, *Conscious Dancer*, *GoDates*, *The Solitude Diaries*, and *Elephant Journal*, where she is also a writing mentor. She has contributed to *The Covid Life Book*, *The Journaling Book* (Routledge), *The Princess and The Pea Collection*, and writes regularly on Substack.

She is also a Tarot reader, and lives in Manchester, UK.

The Story Of The Deer Woman is her debut book.

Heidi offers writing workshops, mentoring, and support for living a creative artist-led life.

To follow her writing adventurings, find Heidi Hinda over at her Substack, Mistress of Words:

https://heidihinda.substack.com/

Instagram: https://www.instagram.com/heidihinda/

About Lemon Jelly Press

Lemon Jelly Press is an independent publisher based on the Isle of Wight, dedicated to championing bold, original voices and beautifully crafted books. With a focus on fiction, poetry, and stories that sit at the edges of the uncanny, the press is committed to nurturing writers, celebrating imagination, and making space for work that lingers long after the final page.

Lemonjellypress.com

As a small publisher, every review, comment and share help us grow.

Please leave your review of this book at

www.goodreads.com
www.lemonjellypress.com
www.amazon.co.uk

Tag us in your posts
@presslemonjelly

Thank you!